THE KILLER
AND OTHER PLAYS

by

Eugène Ionesco

Translated by
Donald Watson

GROVE PRESS, INC. / NEW YORK

EUGÈNE IONESCO

CONTENTS

TRANSLATOR'S NOTE

An attempt has been made to reach a compromise between American and British English, but in the event of production, producers should feel themselves free to change any word that would obviously offend an audience.

Two cases in point would be: elevator/lift and prefect/monitor.

THE KILLER

First produced in Paris by José Quaglio at the Théâtre Récamier, the 27th February, 1959.

CHARACTERS, VOICES, SILHOUETTES
(in order of appearance):

BÉRENGER, an average, middle-aged citizen.

THE ARCHITECT, of ageless, bureaucratic age.

DANY, young typist, conventional pin-up.

THE CLOCHARD, drunk.

THE OWNER OF THE BISTRO, middle-aged, fat, dark and hairy.

ÉDOUARD, 35, thin, nervous, darkly dressed, in mourning.

THE CONCIERGE (preceded by THE VOICE OF THE CONCIERGE), typical concierge. (a woman)

VOICE OF THE CONCIERGE'S DOG.

A MAN'S VOICE.

SECOND MAN'S VOICE.

TRUCK DRIVER'S VOICE.

CAR DRIVER'S VOICE.

FIRST OLD MAN.

SECOND OLD MAN.

THE GROCER.

SCHOOLMASTER'S VOICE.

FIRST VOICE FROM THE STREET.

SECOND VOICE (GRUFF) FROM THE STREET.

THIRD VOICE (PIPING) FROM THE STREET.

FOURTH VOICE FROM THE STREET.

FIRST VOICE FROM BELOW.

SECOND VOICE FROM BELOW.

VOICE FROM THE RIGHT.

Voice from Above.

Voice from the Left.

Second Voice from the Left.

Woman's Voice from the Entrance.

Silhouette of a Motorcyclist on his Bicycle.

Postman's Voice (preceding the Postman himself, if
    desired).

Mother Peep.

Voices of the Crowd.

The Drunk in Top Hat and Tails.

The Old Gentleman with the Little White Beard.

First Policeman.

Second Policeman.

The Echo.

The Killer.

STAGE DIRECTIONS

Several of these parts may be played by the same actors. More-
over, it is probable that all the voices in the second act will not
be heard. Any cuts required may be made in the first half of
Act II: it will all depend on the effectiveness of these voices and
their absurd remarks. The director can choose those he likes.
He should, however, try if possible to obtain stereophonic sound
effects. In the second act it is also better to have the greatest possible number of figures appearing in silhouette the other side of
the window, as on a stage behind the stage. In any case, after the
curtain has risen on the second act, some voices and sounds
around the empty stage are indispensable, at least for a few
minutes, in order to continue and in a way intensify the visual
and aural atmosphere of street and city; this is first created at the
end of Act I, fades after the arrival of Bérenger and returns again
in force at the start of Act III to die right away at the end.

A few cuts could also be made in Act I, according to the power of the actor playing the part and his natural capacity to 'put it over'.

Bérenger's speech to the Killer at the end of the play is one short act in itself. The text should be interpreted in such a way as to bring out the gradual breaking-down of Bérenger, his falling apart and the vacuity of his own rather commonplace morality, which collapses like a leaking balloon. In fact Bérenger finds within himself, in spite of himself and against his own will, arguments in favour of the Killer.

ACT ONE

No decor. An empty stage when the curtain rises. Later there will only be, on the left of the stage, two garden chairs and a table, which the ARCHITECT *will bring on himself. They should be near at hand in the wings.*

The atmosphere for Act I will be created by the lighting only. At first, while the stage is still empty, the light is grey, like a dull November day or afternoon in February. The faint sound of wind; perhaps you can see a dead leaf fluttering across the stage. In the distance the noise of a tram, vague outlines of houses; then, suddenly, the stage is brilliantly lit; a very bright, very white light; just this whiteness, and also the dense vivid blue of the sky. And so, after the grisaille, the lighting effects should simply be made up of white and blue, the only elements in the decor. The noise of the tram, the wind and the rain will have stopped at the very moment the light changes. The blue, the white, the silence and the empty stage should give a strange impression of peace. The audience must be given time to become aware of this. Not until a full minute has passed should the characters appear on the scene.

BÉRENGER *comes on first, from the left, moving quickly. He stops*

in the centre of the stage and turns round briskly to face the
ARCHITECT, *who has followed him more slowly.* BÉRENGER *is
wearing a grey overcoat, hat and scarf. The* ARCHITECT *is in a
summer-weight jacket, light trousers, open-necked shirt and without a hat; under his arm he is carrying a briefcase, rather thick and
heavy, like the one* ÉDOUARD *has in Act II.*

BÉRENGER: Amazing! Amazing! It's extraordinary! As far as I
can see, it's a miracle... [*Vague gesture of protest from the*
ARCHITECT.]... A miracle, or, as I don't suppose you're a
religious man, you'd rather I called it a marvel! I congratulate
you most warmly, it's a marvel, really quite marvellous,
you're a marvellous architect!...
ARCHITECT: Oh... you're very kind...
BÉRENGER: No, no. I *want* to congratulate you. It's absolutely incredible, you've achieved the incredible! The real thing is
quite beyond imagination.
ARCHITECT: It's the work I'm commissioned to do, part of my
normal duties, what I specialize in.
BÉRENGER: Why, yes, of course, to be sure, you're an architect, a
technician and a conscientious civil servant at one and the
same time... Still, that doesn't explain everything. [*Looking
round him and staring at several fixed points on the stage:*] Beautiful,
what a magnificent lawn, that flower-bed!... Oh, what
flowers, appetizing as vegetables, and what vegetables, fragrant
as flowers... and what a blue sky, what an amazingly blue
sky. How wonderful it is! [*To the* ARCHITECT:] In all the
cities of the world, all cities of a certain size, I'm sure there are
civil servants, municipal architects like you, with the same
duties as you, earning the same salary. But they're nowhere
near achieving the same results. [*Gesture of the hand.*] Are you
well paid? I'm sorry, perhaps I'm being indiscreet...
ARCHITECT: Please don't apologize... I'm fairly well paid, the
scale is laid down. It's reasonable... It's all right.

BÉRENGER: But ingenuity like yours is worth its weight in gold. And what's more, I mean the price gold fetched before 1914... the real thing.

ARCHITECT: [*with a modestly disclaiming gesture*] Oh...

BÉRENGER: Oh yes it is... You're the town architect, aren't you?... *Real* gold... After all, today, gold has been devalued, like so many other things, it's paper gold...

ARCHITECT: Your surprise, your...

BÉRENGER: Call it my admiration, my enthusiasm!

ARCHITECT: Very well, your enthusiasm, then, touches me very deeply. I feel I must thank you, dear Monsieur... Bérenger. [*The* ARCHITECT *bows in thanks, after first searching one of his pockets for a card which doubtless bears the name of* BÉRENGER, *and as he bows he reads the name off the card.*]

BÉRENGER: Genuinely enthusiastic, quite genuinely. I'm not the flattering kind, I can tell you.

ARCHITECT: [*ceremoniously, but unimpressed*] I am very highly honoured.

BÉRENGER: It's magnificent! [*He looks about him.*] I'd been told all about it, you see, but I didn't believe it... or rather I wasn't told a thing about it, but I *knew*, I knew that somewhere in our dark and dismal city, in all its mournful, dusty, dirty districts, there was one that was bright and beautiful, this neighbourhood beyond compare, with its sunny streets and avenues bathed in light... this radiant city within a city which you've built...

ARCHITECT: It's a nucleus which is, or rather was, in theory meant to be extended. I planned it all by order of the City Council. I don't allow myself any personal initiative...

BÉRENGER: [*continuing his monologue*] I believed in it, without believing, I knew without knowing! I was afraid to hope... hope, that's not a French word any more, or Turkish, or Polish... Belgian perhaps... and even then...

ARCHITECT: I see, I understand.

BÉRENGER: And yet, *here* I am. Your radiant city is *real*. No doubt of that. You can touch it with your fingers. The blue brilliance of it looks absolutely natural... blue and green... oh, that grass, those rose-pink flowers...

ARCHITECT: Yes, those pink flowers really are roses.

BÉRENGER: Real roses? [*He walks about the stage, pointing, smelling the flowers, etc.*] More blue and more green things too... the colours of joy. And what peace, what peace!

ARCHITECT: That's the rule here, Monsieur... [*He reads off the card:*]... Bérenger. It's all calculated, all intentional. Nothing was to be left to chance in this district, the weather here is always fine. ... And so the building plots always fetch... or rather... always used to fetch a high price... the villas are built of the best materials... built to last, built with care.

BÉRENGER: I don't suppose it ever rains in these houses?

ARCHITECT: Definitely not! That's the least you can expect. Does it rain in yours?

BÉRENGER: Yes, I'm afraid it does.

ARCHITECT: It oughtn't to, even in your district. I'll send a man round.

BÉRENGER: Well, I suppose it doesn't really rain *inside*. Only in a manner of speaking. It's so damp, it's as if it *was* raining.

ARCHITECT: I see. Morally speaking. In any case, here in this district it never rains at all. And yet all the walls and all the roofs of the buildings you can see are damp-proof. It's a habit, a matter of form. Quite unnecessary, but it keeps up an old tradition.

BÉRENGER: You say it *never* rains? And all these things growing? This grass? And not a dead leaf on the trees, not a faded flower in the garden!

ARCHITECT: They're watered from below.

BÉRENGER: A technical marvel! Forgive me for being so astonished, a layman like me... [*With his handkrcheief he is mopping the sweat from his brow.*]

ARCHITECT: Why don't you take your overcoat off? Carry it on your arm, you're too hot.

BÉRENGER: Why yes... I'm not at all cold any more... Thank you, thanks for the suggestion. [*He takes off his overcoat and puts it over his arm; he keeps his hat on his head. He looks up, with a gesture:*] The leaves on the trees are small enough for the light to filter through, but not too big, so as not to darken the front of the houses. I must say it's amazing to think that in all the rest of the town the sky's as grey as the hair on an old woman's head, that there's dirty snow at the pavements' edge, and the wind blowing there. When I woke up this morning I was very cold. I was frozen. The radiators work so badly in my block of flats, especially on the ground-floor. They work even worse when they don't make up the fire... So I mean to say...

[*A telephone bell rings, coming from the* ARCHITECT*'s pocket; the* ARCHITECT *takes a receiver from it and listens; the telephone wire ends in his pocket.*]

ARCHITECT: Hullo?

BÉRENGER: Forgive me, Monsieur, I'm keeping you from your work...

ARCHITECT: [*to telephone*] Hullo? [*To* BÉRENGER:] Not a bit... I've kept an hour free to show you the district. No trouble at all. [*To telephone:*] Hullo? Yes. I know about that. Let the assistant manager know. Right. Let him hold an investigation if he insists. *He* can make the official arrangements. I'm with Monsieur Bérenger, for the visit to the radiant city. [*He puts the machine back in his pocket. To* BÉRENGER, *who has taken a few steps away, lost in admiration:*] You were saying? Hey, where are you?

BÉRENGER: Here. I'm sorry. What was I saying? Oh yes... Oh, it doesn't really matter now.

ARCHITECT: Go ahead. Say it anyway.

BÉRENGER: I was saying... oh yes... in my district, especially where I live, everything is damp; the coal, the bread, the wind, the wine, the walls, the air, and even the fire. What a job I had this morning, getting up, I had to make a big effort.

It was really painful. I'd never have made up my mind if the sheets hadn't been damp too. I never imagined that, suddenly, as if by magic, I should find myself in the midst of spring, in the middle of April, the April of my dreams... my earliest dreams...

ARCHITECT: Dreams! [*Shrugging his shoulders.*] Anyhow, it would have been better if you'd come sooner, come before...

BÉRENGER: [*interrupting him*] Ah yes, I've lost a lot of time, that's true...

[BÉRENGER *and the* ARCHITECT *go on walking about the stage.* BÉRENGER *should give the impression he is walking through tree-lined avenues and parks. The* ARCHITECT *follows him, more slowly. At times* BÉRENGER *will have to turn round to speak to the* ARCHITECT *in a louder voice. He should appear to be waiting for the* ARCHITECT *to come closer. Pointing to empty space:*]

BÉRENGER: *There's* an attractive house! The façade is delightful, such a wonderfully pure style. 18th century? No, 15th or the end of the 19th? It's classical anyway, and then it's so neat, so smart... Ah yes, I've lost a lot of time, is it too late?... No... Yes... No, it may not be too late, what do you think?

ARCHITECT: I haven't given the matter much thought.

BÉRENGER: I'm thirty-five years old, Monsieur, thirty-five... Actually to tell the truth, I'm forty, forty-five, perhaps a little more.

ARCHITECT: [*consulting the card*] We know. Your age is on the card. We have files on everyone.

BÉRENGER: Really? Oh!

ARCHITECT: It's quite usual, we have to have them for the record, but don't worry, the code provides no penalties for that kind of prevarication, not for vanity.

BÉRENGER: Thank goodness for that! Anyway, if I only admit to thirty-five, it's certainly not to deceive my fellow citizens, what's it matter to them? It's to deceive myself. In this way I act on myself by suggestion, I believe myself to be younger, I cheer myself up...

ARCHITECT: It's only human, only natural. [*The pocket telephone rings; the* ARCHITECT *takes it out again.*]

BÉRENGER: Oh, what nice little stones on the paths!

ARCHITECT: [*to telephone*] Hullo?... A woman? Take a description of her. Enter it up. Send it to the statistics department...

BÉRENGER: [*pointing to the corner of the stage on the left*] What's that over there?

ARCHITECT: [*to telephone*] No, no, no, nothing else to report. All the time *I'm* here, nothing else *can* happen. [*He puts the receiver back in his pocket. To* BÉRENGER:] I'm sorry, I'm listening now.

BÉRENGER: [*as before*] What's that over there?

ARCHITECT: Oh, that... It's a greenhouse.

BÉRENGER: A greenhouse?

ARCHITECT: Yes. For the flowers that can't get used to a temperate climate, the flowers that like the cold. We've created a wintry climate for them. Now and again we have a little storm...

BÉRENGER: Ah, everything's been thought of... yes, Monsieur, I could be sixty years old, seventy, eighty, a hundred and twenty, how do I know?

ARCHITECT: Morally speaking!

BÉRENGER: It can be interpreted physically too. It's psychosomatic... Am I talking nonsense?

ARCHITECT: Not particularly. Like everyone else.

BÉRENGER: I feel old. Time is above all subjective. Or rather I *used* to feel old. Since this morning I'm a new man. I'm sure I'm becoming myself again. The world's becoming itself again; it's all thanks to *your* power. Your magic light...

ARCHITECT: My electric light!

BÉRENGER: ... Your radiant city. [*He points quite near.*] It's the power of those immaculate walls covered with roses, your masterpiece! Ah, yes, yes, yes!... nothing's really lost, I'm sure of that now... Now, in fact, I *do* remember, two or three people did tell me about the smiling city; some said it was quite near, others that it was far away, that it was easy to get to, hard to find, that it was a district specially reserved...

ARCHITECT: Not true!

BÉRENGER: ... That there was no means of transport...

ARCHITECT: Nonsense. There's a tram stop over there, at the end of the main thoroughfare.

BÉRENGER: Yes, of course, of course! I know *now*. For a long time, I tell you, I tried consciously or unconsciously to find the way. I would walk right to the end of a street, and then realize it was a dead end. I'd follow a wall or a fence until I reached the river far from the bridge, away beyond the market and the gates of the town. Or else I'd meet some friends on the way, who hadn't seen me since our army days; I'd be forced to stop and chat to them until it was too late and I had to go home. Still, what does it matter now? I'm *here*. My worries are over.

ARCHITECT: It was really so simple. You only had to drop me a line, write an official letter to the municipal offices, and one of my departments would have sent you all the necessary information by registered post.

BÉRENGER: Why yes, I only needed to think of that! Oh well, no good crying over lost years...

ARCHITECT: How did you set about finding the way today?

BÉRENGER: Pure accident. I just took the tram.

ARCHITECT: What did I tell you?

BÉRENGER: Took the wrong tram, I meant to take another, I was sure it wasn't going the right way, and yet it *was*, by mistake, a lucky mistake...

ARCHITECT: Lucky?

BÉRENGER: No? Not lucky? But it *was*. Very, very lucky.

ARCHITECT: Oh well, you'll see for yourself, later.

BÉRENGER: I've seen already. I'm firmly convinced.

ARCHITECT: Anyway, remember you must always go as far as the terminus. Whatever the circumstances. All trams lead this way: it's the depot.

BÉRENGER: I know. The tram brought me here, to this stop. Although I hadn't been here before, I recognized everything at once; the avenues and the houses all blossoming, and you, looking as if you expected me.

ARCHITECT: I'd been informed.

BÉRENGER: It's such a transformation! It's as though I was far away in the South, two or three thousand miles away. Another universe, a world transfigured! And just that very short journey to get here, a journey that isn't *really*, since you might say it takes place in the same place... [*He laughs; then embarrassed:*] Forgive me, that wasn't very funny.

ARCHITECT: Don't look so upset. I've heard worse. I'll put it down to your state of bliss...

BÉRENGER: I've no mind for science. I suppose that's why in spite of your very pertinent explanations, *I* can't explain how the weather can always be fine here! Perhaps—this may have made it easier for you—perhaps it's a more sheltered spot? And yet it's not surrounded by hills to protect it from bad weather! Besides, hills don't chase the clouds away or stop it raining, everyone knows that. Is it that there are bright warm waves of air coming from a fifth point of the compass or some third stratum of the upper air? No, I suppose there aren't. Everyone would know about it. I'm really stupid. There's no breeze, although the air smells good. I must say it's odd, Monsieur, it's very odd!

ARCHITECT: [*giving the authoritative information*] I tell you there's nothing unusual about it, it's a technical matter! So try and understand. You ought to have taken an Adult Education Course. It's just that this is a little island... with concealed ventilators I copied from the ones in those oases that crop up all over the place in the desert, where suddenly out of the dry sand you see amazing cities rising up, smothered with dewy roses, girdled with springs and rivers and lakes...

BÉRENGER: Oh yes... That's true. You mean those cities that are also called mirages. I've read explorers' tales about them.

You see, I'm not completely uneducated. Mirages... there's nothing more real than a mirage. Flowers on fire, trees in flame, pools of light, that's all there really is that matters. I'm sure of it. And over there? What's that?

ARCHITECT: Over where? Where? Oh, over there?

BÉRENGER: Looks like an ornamental pool.

[*By means of the lighting, the vague outline of an ornamental pool appears at the back of the stage just as he says these words.*]

ARCHITECT: Er... yes, it *is* a pool. You recognized it. It's a pool, all right. [*He consults his watch.*] I think I still have a few minutes.

BÉRENGER: Can we go and see?

ARCHITECT: You want to have a closer look? [*He appears to hesitate.*] Very well. If you insist, I'll have to show it you.

BÉRENGER: Or instead... I don't know what to choose... It's all so beautiful... I like ornamental pools, but I rather like the look of that flowering hawthorn too. If you don't mind, we can look at the pool later...

ARCHITECT: As you like.

BÉRENGER: I love hawthorn bushes.

ARCHITECT: You've only to make up your mind.

BÉRENGER: Yes, yes, let's go over to the hawthorn.

ARCHITECT: I'm completely at your service.

BÉRENGER: One can't see everything at once.

ARCHITECT: True enough.

[*The pool disappears. They walk a few steps.*]

BÉRENGER: What a sweet smell! You know, Monsieur, I... forgive me for talking about myself... one can say anything to an architect, he understands everything.

ARCHITECT: Do please carry on. Don't be shy.

BÉRENGER: Thank you! You know, I do so need another life, a new life. Different surroundings, a different setting. A different setting, you'll think that's not much to ask, and that...with money, for example..

ARCHITECT: No, not at all...

BÉRENGER: Yes, yes, you're too polite... A setting, *that's* just superficial, an artistic consideration, unless it's, how shall I say, a setting, a background that would answer some profound need inside, which would be somehow...

ARCHITECT: I see, I see...

BÉRENGER: ... the projection, the continuation of the universe inside you. Only, to project this universe within, some outside help is needed: some kind of material, physical light, a world that is objectively new. Gardens, blue sky, or the spring, which corresponds to the universe inside and offers a chance of recognition, which is like a translation or an anticipation of that universe, or a mirror in which its own smile could be reflected... in which it can find itself again and say: that's what I am in reality and I'd forgotten, a smiling being in a smiling world... Come to think of it, it's quite wrong to talk of a world within and a world without, separate worlds; there's an initial impulse, of course, which starts from us, and when it can't project itself, when it can't fulfil itself objectively, when there's not total agreement between myself inside and myself outside, then it's a catastrophe, a universal contradiction, a schism.

ARCHITECT: [scratching his head] What a vocabulary you have. We don't talk the same language.

BÉRENGER: I felt I couldn't go on living, and yet I couldn't die. Luckily it's all going to be different now.

ARCHITECT: Don't get too excited!

BÉRENGER: I'm sorry. I get carried away.

ARCHITECT: That's characteristic of you. You're one of those poetic personalities. As they exist, I suppose they must be necessary.

BÉRENGER: Year after year of dirty snow and bitter winds, of a climate indifferent to human beings... streets and houses and whole districts of people who aren't really unhappy, but worse, who are neither happy nor unhappy, people who are ugly because they're neither ugly nor beautiful, creatures that are dismally neutral, who long without longings as though they're unconscious, unconsciously suffering from being alive. But *I* was aware of the sickness of life. Perhaps because I'm more intelligent, or just the opposite, *less* intelligent, not so wise, not so resigned, not so patient. Is that a fault or a virtue?

ARCHITECT: [*giving signs of impatience*] Depends.

BÉRENGER: You can't tell. The winter of the soul! I'm not expressing myself clearly, am I?

ARCHITECT: I'm not capable of judging. It's not one of my duties. The logic department sees to that.

BÉRENGER: Perhaps you don't appreciate my lyrical side?

ARCHITECT: [*dryly*] Why yes, of course!

BÉRENGER: Well, you see: once upon a time there was a blazing fire inside me. The cold could do nothing against it, a youthfulness, a spring no autumn could touch; a source of light, glowing wells of joy that seemed inexhaustible. Not happiness, I mean joy, felicity, which made it possible for me to live...

[*The telephone rings in the* ARCHITECT'*s pocket.*]

There was enormous energy there...

[*The* ARCHITECT *takes the telephone from his pocket.*]

A force... it must have been the life force, mustn't it?

ARCHITECT: [*holding the receiver to his ear*] Hullo?

BÉRENGER: And then it grew weaker and all died away.

ARCHITECT; [*to the telephone*] Hullo? Fine, fine, fine!... Don't tell me that only happened yesterday!

BÉRENGER: [*continuing his monologue*] Oh it must go back... I don't know how long... a long, long time ago...

[*The* ARCHITECT *puts the receiver back in his pocket and shows fresh signs of impatience; he goes into the wings on the left and brings on a chair, which he sets down in the left-hand corner, where the greenhouse was supposed to be.*]

Must be centuries ago... or perhaps only a few years, perhaps it was yesterday...

ARCHITECT: I must ask you to excuse me, I'm afraid I must go to my office. I've some urgent matters to attend to. [*He goes off left for a moment.*]

BÉRENGER: [*alone*] Oh... Monsieur, really, I'm so sorry, I...

ARCHITECT: [*coming back with a small table, which he sets in front of the chair; he sits down, takes the telephone from his pocket, puts it on the table and lays his briefcase open before him*] It's for me to apologize.

BÉRENGER: Oh, no! I feel terrible about it!

ARCHITECT: Don't let it upset you too much. I have two ears; one for duty, and the other I reserve for you. One eye too, for you. The other's for the borough.

BÉRENGER: It won't tire you too much?

ARCHITECT: Don't worry. I'm used to it. All right, carry on... [*He takes from his briefcase, or pretends to, some files which he lays out on the table and opens.*] I'm attending to my files, and to you too... You were saying you didn't know how long ago it was this force died away!

BÉRENGER: It certainly wasn't yesterday. [*He goes on walking, from now on, round and round the* ARCHITECT, *who is plunged in his files.*] It's such an old story, I've almost forgotten, it might have been an illusion; and yet it can't be an illusion when I still feel the loss of it so badly.

ARCHITECT: [*in his files*] Go on.

BÉRENGER: I can't analyse the feeling, I don't even know if the experience I had can be communicated. It wasn't very frequent. It happened, five or six, ten times perhaps in my life. Often enough, though, to fill to overflowing Heaven knows what secret reservoirs of my mind with joy and conviction. When I was in a gloomy mood, the memory of that dazzling radiance, that glowing feeling, gave fresh life to the force within me, to those reasonless reasons for living and loving... loving what?... Loving everything wholeheartedly...

ARCHITECT: [*to the telephone*] Hullo, the supplies have run out!

BÉRENGER: Yes, I'm afraid they have, Monsieur.

ARCHITECT: [*who has hung up*] I wasn't saying that to you, it's about my files.

BÉRENGER: It's true for me too, Monsieur, the reservoirs are empty. I'm not economically sound any more. My supplies of light have run out. I'll try and explain... I'm not imposing on you?

ARCHITECT: It's going in the record. That's my job. Carry on, don't mind me.

BÉRENGER: It happened as spring was ending, or perhaps in the very first days of summer, just before midday; it all came about in a way that was perfectly simple and perfectly unexpected as well. The sky was as pure as the one you've managed to cover your radiant city with, Monsieur. Yes, it happened in extraordinary silence, in a long, long second of silence...

ARCHITECT: [still in his files] Right. Fine.

BÉRENGER: The last time I must have been seventeen or eighteen, and I was in a little country town... which one?... I wonder which it was?... Somewhere in the South, I think... It's of no importance anyway, the place hardly counts. I was walking along a narrow street, which was both old and new, with low houses on either side, all white and tucked away in courtyards or little gardens, with wooden fences, painted... pale yellow, was it pale yellow? I was all alone in the street. I was walking along by the fences and the houses, and it was fine, not too hot, with the sun above, high above my head in the blue of the sky. I was walking fast, but where was I going? I don't remember. I was deeply aware of the unique joy of being alive. I'd forgotten everything, all I could think of was those houses, that deep sky and that sun, which seemed to be coming nearer, within my grasp, in a world that was made for me.

ARCHITECT: [consulting his watch] She's not here yet! Late again!

BÉRENGER: [continuing] Suddenly the joy became more intense, breaking all bounds! And then, oh what indescribable bliss took hold of me! The light grew more and more brilliant, and still lost none of its softness, it was so dense you could almost breathe it, it had become the air itself, you could drink it like clear water... How can I convey its incomparable brilliance?... It's as if there were four suns in the sky...

ARCHITECT: [*speaking into the telephone*] Hullo? Have you seen my secretary today? There's a pile of work waiting. [*He hangs up angrily.*]

BÉRENGER: The houses I was passing were like immaterial shades ready to melt away in that mightier light which governed all.

ARCHITECT: I'll make her pay a nice fat fine!

BÉRENGER: [*to* ARCHITECT] You see what I mean?

ARCHITECT: [*vaguely*] More or less. Your story seems clearer now.

BÉRENGER: Not a man in the street, not a cat, not a sound, there was only me.

[*The telephone bell rings.*]

And yet I didn't suffer from being alone, I didn't feel lonely.

ARCHITECT: [*to the telephone*] Well, has she arrived?

BÉRENGER: My own peace and light spread in their turn throughout the world, I was filling the universe with a kind of ethereal energy. Not an empty corner, everything was a mingling of airiness and plenitude, perfectly balanced.

ARCHITECT: [*to the telephone*] At last! Put her on the line.

BÉRENGER: A song of triumph rose from the depths of my being: I *was*, I realized I had always *been*, that I was no longer going to die.

ARCHITECT: [*on the telephone, mastering his irritation*] I must say I'm very pleased to hear your voice, Mademoiselle. It's about time. What?

BÉRENGER: Everything was virgin, purified, discovered anew. I had a feeling of inexpressible surprise, yet at the same time it was all quite familiar to me.

ARCHITECT: [*on the telephone*] What do you mean by that, Mademoiselle?

BÉRENGER: That's *it* all right, I said to myself, that's *it*, all right... I can't tell *you* what I mean by 'it', but I promise you, Monsieur *I* understood quite well what I meant.

ARCHITECT: [*on the telephone*] I don't understand you, Mademoiselle. You've no reason to be dissatisfied with us, I should say the boot's on the other foot.

BÉRENGER: I felt I was there at the gates, at the very centre of the universe... That must seem contradictory to you?

ARCHITECT: [*on the telephone*] One moment, please. [*To* BÉRENGER:] I follow you, I follow you, don't worry, I get the general idea. [*On the telephone:*] Hullo, yes?

BÉRENGER: I walked and ran and cried: I *am*, I *am*, *everything* is, everything *is!*... Oh, I'm sure I could have flown away, I'd lost so much weight, I was lighter than the blue sky I was breathing... The slightest effort, the tiniest little leap would have been enough... I should have taken off... I'm sure I should.

ARCHITECT: [*on the telephone, banging his fist on the table*] Now that's going too far! What's made you feel like this?

BÉRENGER: If I didn't do it, it's because I was too happy, it didn't even enter my head.

ARCHITECT: [*on the telephone*] You want to leave the Service? Think carefully before you resign. Without any good reason you're abandoning a brilliant career! After all, with us your future is insured, *and* your life... your life! You aren't afraid of the danger!

BÉRENGER: And suddenly, or rather gradually... no, it was all at once, I don't know, I only know that everything went grey and pale and neutral again. Not really, of course, the sky was still pure, but it wasn't the same purity, it wasn't the same sun, the same morning, the same spring. It was like a conjuring trick. The light was the same as on any other day, ordinary daylight.

ARCHITECT: [*on the telephone*] You can't stand the situation any longer? That's childish. I refuse your resignation. Come and clear up the day's mail anyway, and you can explain yourself. I'm waiting for you. [*He hangs up.*]

BÉRENGER: There was a kind of chaotic vacuum inside me, I was overcome with the immense sadness you feel at a moment of tragic and intolerable separation. The old gossips came out of their courtyards and split my eardrums with their screeching voices, the dogs barked, and I felt lost among all those people, all those *things*...

ARCHITECT: She's a stupid girl. [*He stands up.*] Still, it's her own affair. There are thousands more after her job... [*He sits down again.*]... and a life without peril.

BÉRENGER: And since then, it's been perpetual November, perpetual twilight, twilight in the morning, twilight at midnight, twilight at noon. The light of dawn has gone! And to think we call this civilization!

ARCHITECT: We're still waiting!

BÉRENGER: It's only the memory of what happened that's helped me to go on living in this grey city.

ARCHITECT: [*to* BÉRENGER] You got over it, just the same, this... melancholy?

BÉRENGER: Not entirely. But I promised myself I wouldn't forget. I told myself that on the days I felt sad and nervous, depressed and anxious, I would always remember that glorious moment. It would help me to bear everything, give me a reason for living, and be a comfort to me. For years I felt sure...

ARCHITECT: Sure of what?

BÉRENGER: Sure I'd been sure... but the memory wasn't strong enough to stand the test of time.

ARCHITECT: But it seems to me...

BÉRENGER: You're wrong, Monsieur. The memory I've kept is nothing now but the memory of a memory, like a thought grown foreign to me, like a tale told by another, a faded picture whose brightness I could no longer restore. The water in the well had dried up and I was dying of thirst... But *you* must understand me perfectly, this light is in *you* too, it's the same as mine, because [*A broad gesture taking in empty space.*] you have obviously recreated and materialized it. This radiant district must have sprung from you... You've given me back that forgotten light... almost. I'm terribly grateful to you. In my name and in the name of all who live here, I thank you.

ARCHITECT: Why yes, of course.

BÉRENGER: And with you, it's not the unreal product of an over-
heated imagination. These are real houses and stones and bricks
and cement. [*Touching empty space.*] It's concrete, solid,
tangible. Yours is the right system, your methods are rational.
[*He still appears to be feeling the walls.*]

ARCHITECT: [*also feeling the invisible walls, after leaving his corner*]
It's brick, yes, and good brick too. Cement, the best quality.

BÉRENGER: [*as before*] No, no, it's not just a dream, this time.

ARCHITECT: [*still feeling the invisible walls, then stopping with a
sigh*] Perhaps it would have been better if it had been a dream.
It's all the same to me. I'm a civil servant. But for a lot of other
people, reality, unlike dreams, can turn into a nightmare...

BÉRENGER: [*who also stops feeling the invisible walls, greatly surprised*] Why, what do you mean?
[*The ARCHITECT returns to his files.*]
In any case, I'm glad my memory is real and I can feel it with
my fingers. I'm as young as I was a hundred years ago. I can
fall in love again... [*Calling to the wings on the right:*] Mademoiselle, oh, Mademoiselle, will you marry me?
[*Just as he finishes this last sentence, DANY comes in from the right.
She is the ARCHITECT's blonde secretary.*]

ARCHITECT: [*to DANY as she enters*] Oh, so there you are! I've
got something to say to you!

DANY: [*To BÉRENGER*] Do give me time to think it over!

ARCHITECT: [*to BÉRENGER*] My secretary, Mademoiselle Dany.
[*To DANY:*] Monsieur Bérenger.

DANY: [*absentmindedly, rather nervously, to BÉRENGER*] Pleased to
meet you.

ARCHITECT: [*to DANY*] In the Civil Service we don't like people
to be late, Mademoiselle, or impulsive either.

BÉRENGER: [*to DANY, who goes and sets her typewriter on the table,
and fetches a chair from the wings on the left*] Mademoiselle Dany,
what a lovely name! Have you thought it over yet? The

answer's 'Yes' isn't it?

DANY: [*to the* ARCHITECT] I've made up my mind to leave, Monsieur, I need a holiday, I'm tired.

ARCHITECT: [*sweetly*] If that's all it is, you should have told me. We can arrange something. Would you like three days off?

BÉRENGER: [*to* DANY] It is Yes, isn't it? Oh, you're so beautiful.

DANY: [*to* ARCHITECT] I must have a much longer rest than that.

ARCHITECT: [*to* DANY] I'll apply to the Departmental Board, I can get you a week—half-pay.

DANY: [*to* ARCHITECT] I need a permanent rest.

BÉRENGER: [*to* DANY] I like fair girls, with glowing faces, bright eyes and long legs!

ARCHITECT: Permanent? I see!...

DANY: [*to* ARCHITECT] I simply must do some different work. I can't stand the situation any longer.

ARCHITECT: Oh, so that's it.

DANY: [*to* ARCHITECT] Yes, Monsieur.

BÉRENGER: [*to* DANY, *enthusiastically*] You said Yes! Oh, Mademoiselle Dany...

ARCHITECT: [*to* BÉRENGER] She's talking to me, not to you.

DANY: [*to* ARCHITECT] I always hoped things might change, but they're still the same. I don't see any chance of improvement.

ARCHITECT: Now think, I'm telling you again, think carefully! If you no longer belong to our organization, the Civil Service can no longer take you under its wing. Do you realize? Are you fully aware of the dangers that lie in wait?

DANY: Yes, Monsieur, no one's in a better position than I am to know about that.

ARCHITECT: You're willing to take the risk?

DANY: [*to* ARCHITECT] I am, yes, Monsieur.

BÉRENGER: [*to* DANY] Say Yes to me too. You say it so nicely.

ARCHITECT: [*to* DANY] Then I refuse all responsibility. You have been warned.

DANY: [*to* ARCHITECT] I'm not deaf, I understand, you needn't repeat yourself!

BÉRENGER: [*to* ARCHITECT] Isn't she sweet! Delightful. [*To* DANY:] Mademoiselle, Mademoiselle, we'll live here, in this district, in this villa! We'll be happy at last.

ARCHITECT: [*to* DANY] So you really won't change your mind? It's a crazy, headstrong thing to do!

DANY: [*to* ARCHITECT] No, Monsieur.

BÉRENGER: [*to* DANY] Oh, you didn't say No?

ARCHITECT: [*to* BÉRENGER] She said No to *me*.

BÉRENGER: Ah, that's all right, then!

DANY: [*to* ARCHITECT] I hate the Civil Service, I detest your beautiful district, I can't stand any more, I can't bear it!

ARCHITECT: [*to* DANY] It's not *my* district.

BÉRENGER: [*to* DANY, *who is not listening*] Give me your answer, beautiful Demoiselle, Dany the magnificent, Dany the sublime... May I call you Dany?

ARCHITECT: [*to* DANY] I can't stop you resigning, so you'd better go, but keep a sharp look-out. That's a piece of friendly advice I'm giving you, fatherly advice.

BÉRENGER: [*to* ARCHITECT] Were you decorated for your achievements in urban development? You should have been.

DANY: [*to* ARCHITECT] If you like, I'll finish typing the letters before I go.

BÉRENGER: [*to* ARCHITECT] If I'd been the Mayor, I'd have decorated you all right.

ARCHITECT: [*to* BÉRENGER] Thank you. [*To* DANY:] You needn't bother, thank you. I'll manage.

BÉRENGER: [*smelling imaginary flowers*] What a lovely smell! Are they lilies?

ARCHITECT: No, violets.

DANY: [*to* ARCHITECT] I was only trying to be helpful.

BÉRENGER: [*to* ARCHITECT] May I pick some for Dany?

ARCHITECT: If you like.

BÉRENGER: [*to* DANY] You don't know, my dear, dear Dany, dear fiancée, how I've longed for you.

DANY: If that's how you take it... [*In some irritation she briskly puts her things in order and picks up her typewriter.*]

BÉRENGER: [*to* DANY] We'll live in a wonderful flat, full of sunshine.

DANY: [*to* ARCHITECT] Surely you can understand I can't go on sharing the responsibility. It's too much for me.

ARCHITECT: The Civil Service is not responsible for that.

DANY: [*to* ARCHITECT] You ought to be able to realize...

ARCHITECT: [*to* DANY] It's not for you to give *me* advice. That's *my* business. But I warn you again; watch your step.

DANY: [*to* ARCHITECT] I'm not taking advice from you either. It's *my* business too.

ARCHITECT: [*to* DANY] All right, all right!

DANY: Au revoir, Monsieur.

ARCHITECT: Goodbye.

DANY: [*to* BÉRENGER] Au revoir, Monsieur.

BÉRENGER: [*running after* DANY, *who is making for the exit on the right*] Dany, Mademoiselle, don't go before you've given me an answer... At least, please take these violets.

[DANY *goes out.* BÉRENGER *stands near the exit, his arms hanging loosely.*]

Oh... [*To* ARCHITECT:] You understand the human heart; when a woman doesn't answer Yes or No, it means Yes, doesn't it? [*Calling towards the wings on the right:*] You'll be my inspiration, my Muse. I'll really *work.* [*While a slight echo is heard repeating the previous words,* BÉRENGER *moves two paces nearer the* ARCHITECT *and indicates the empty space:*] I'll not give up. I'm settling down here with Dany. I'll buy that white house, with the trees and grass all round, the one that looks abandoned by the builders... I haven't much money, you'll let me pay in instalments.

ARCHITECT: If you really want to! If you're not going to change your mind.

BÉRENGER: I'm determined. Why should I change my mind? With your permission, I want to be a citizen of the radiant city. I'll move in tomorrow, even if the house isn't quite ready yet.

ARCHITECT: [*looking at his watch*] Twenty-five to one.

[*Suddenly, there is the noise of a stone falling a few paces from BÉRENGER, between him and the ARCHITECT.*]

BÉRENGER: Oh! [*Starts back a little.*] A stone!

ARCHITECT: [*impassively, without surprise*] Yes, a stone!

BÉRENGER: [*leans forward and picks up the stone, then straightens up and inspects it in his hand*] It *is* a stone!

ARCHITECT: Haven't you seen one before?

BÉRENGER: Yes... of course... What? They're throwing stones at us?

ARCHITECT: *A* stone, just one stone, not stones!

BÉRENGER: I understand, they threw a stone at us.

ARCHITECT: Don't worry. They're not really going to stone you. It didn't touch you, did it?

BÉRENGER: It could have.

ARCHITECT: No, no, of course it couldn't. It *cannot* touch you. It's only teasing.

BÉRENGER: Oh, I see!... If it's only teasing, then I suppose I can take a joke! [*He drops the stone.*] I don't easily take offence. Especially in these surroundings it takes a lot to upset you. She will write to me, won't she? [*He casts a rather anxious look about him.*] It's so restful here, and intended to be that way. Almost a little too restful, don't you think? Why can't you see a single soul in the streets? We really are the only people out!... Oh yes, of course, it must be because it's lunchtime. Everyone's eating. But why can't we hear any laughter at table, any clinking of glasses? Not a sound, not a whisper, not a voice singing. And all the windows are shut! [*He looks round the empty stage, surprised.*] I didn't notice before. It would be understandable in a dream, but not when it's real.

ARCHITECT: I'd have thought it was obvious.

[*The sound of broken window-panes is heard.*]

BÉRENGER: What's happening now?

ARCHITECT: [*taking the telephone from his pocket again ; to BÉRENGER*]

That's easy. You don't know what it is? A window's been smashed. It must have been broken by a stone.

[*The noise of another window being smashed;* BÉRENGER *starts back more violently. On the telephone :*] Two broken windows.

BÉRENGER: What's it all about? A joke, I suppose? Two jokes! [*Another stone knocks his hat off; he picks the hat up quickly and puts it back on his head.*] Three jokes!

ARCHITECT: [*putting the telephone back in his pocket and frowning*] Now listen, Monsieur. You and I are not business men. We're civil servants, bureaucrats. So I must tell you officially, bureaucratically, that the house that looked abandoned really has been abandoned by the builders. The police have suspended all construction work. I knew this before, but I've just had it confirmed by phone.

BÉRENGER: What?... Why?

ARCHITECT: It's an unnecessary step to take anyway. You're the only one wants to buy any property now. I don't suppose you know what it's all about...

BÉRENGER: What *is* it all about?

ARCHITECT: Actually, the people who live in this district want to leave it...

BÉRENGER: Leave the radiant district? The people want to leave it...

ARCHITECT: Yes. They've no other homes to go to. Otherwise they'd *all* have packed their bags. Perhaps too they make it a point of honour not to run away. They'd rather stay and hide in their beautiful flats. They only come out when they really have to, in groups of ten or fifteen at a time. And even that doesn't make for safety...

BÉRENGER: What's so dangerous? Just another joke, isn't it! Why are you looking so serious? You're clouding the whole place over! You're trying to frighten me!...

ARCHITECT: [*solemnly*] A civil servant doesn't make jokes.

BÉRENGER: [*terribly upset*] What are you talking about? You're really upsetting me! It's you who just threw that stone at me...

Morally speaking of course! Oh dear, and I already felt I'd taken root in these surroundings! Now all the brilliance they offer is dead, and they're nothing more than an empty frame... I feel shut out!

ARCHITECT: I'm very sorry. Steady there!

BÉRENGER: I've a horrible premonition.

ARCHITECT: I'm so sorry, so sorry.

[*During the previous dialogue and what comes after, the acting should never lose a touch of irony, which should especially balance the pathetic moments.*]

BÉRENGER: I can feel the darkness spreading inside me again!

ARCHITECT: [*dryly*] Sorry, very sorry, so sorry.

BÉRENGER: Please, you must explain. I was so hoping to spend a nice day!... I was so happy a few moments ago.

ARCHITECT: [*pointing*] You see this ornamental pool?

[*The pool reappears, clearly this time.*]

BÉRENGER: It's the same one we went past already, just now!

ARCHITECT: I wanted to show you then... You preferred the hawthorns... [*He points to the pool again :*] It's there in the pool every day, that two or three people are found, drowned.

BÉRENGER: Drowned?

ARCHITECT: Come and look if you don't believe me. Come on, come closer!

BÉRENGER: [*accompanying the* ARCHITECT *to the place indicated or right to the front of the stage, while the objects referred to appear as they are mentioned*] Go nearer!

ARCHITECT: Look! What do you see?

BÉRENGER: Oh, Heavens!

ARCHITECT: Come on now, no fainting, be a man!

BÉRENGER: [*with an effort*] I can see... it's not true... Yes, I can see, on the water, the dead body of a little boy, floating in his hoop... a little chap of five or six... He's clutching the stick in his hand... Next to him the bloated corpse of an officer in the engineers in full uniform...

ARCHITECT: There are even three today. [*Pointing*] Over there!

BÉRENGER: It's a plant in the water!

ARCHITECT: Look again.

BÉRENGER: Good God!... Yes... I see! It's red hair streaming up from the bottom, stuck to the marble edge of the pool. How horrible! It must be a woman.

ARCHITECT: [*shrugging his shoulders*] Obviously. And one's a man. And the other's a child. *We* don't know any more than that, either.

BÉRENGER: Perhaps it's the boy's mother! Poor devils! Why didn't you tell me before?

ARCHITECT: But I told you! You were always stopping me, always admiring the beautiful surroundings.

BÉRENGER: Poor devils! [*Violently*] Who did it?

ARCHITECT: The murderer, the thug. Always the same elusive character.

BÉRENGER: But our lives are in danger! Let's go! [*He takes to his heels, runs a few yards across the stage and comes back to the* ARCHITECT, *who has not moved.*] Let's go! [*He takes flight again, but runs round and round the* ARCHITECT, *who takes out a cigarette and lights it. A shot is heard.*] He's shooting!

ARCHITECT: Don't be afraid. You're in no danger while you're with me.

BÉRENGER: What about that shot? Oh, no... no... You don't make me feel safer! [*He moves restlessly about and starts shaking.*]

ARCHITECT: It's only a game... Yes... Just now, it's only a game, to tease you! I'm the City Architect, a municipal civil servant, he doesn't attack the Civil Service. When I've retired, it'll be different, but for the moment...

BÉRENGER: Let's go. Get away from here. I can't wait to leave your beautiful district...

ARCHITECT: There you are, you see, you *have* changed your mind!

BÉRENGER: You mustn't hold it against me!

ARCHITECT: I don't care. I haven't been asked to detail volunteers and compel them to live here by choice. No one's obliged to live dangerously if he doesn't want that sort of life!... When the district's completely depopulated, they'll pull it down.

BÉRENGER: [still hurrying round and round the ARCHITECT] Depopulated?

ARCHITECT: People will decide to leave it in the end... or they'll all be killed. Oh, it'll take a bit of time...

BÉRENGER: Let's be off, quick! [He goes round and round, faster and faster, with his head well down.] The rich aren't always happy either, nor are the people who live in the residential districts... or the radiant ones... There are no radiant ones!... It's even worse than the other districts, in ours, the busy crowded ones!... Oh, Monsieur, I feel so upset about it. I feel shattered, stunned... My tiredness has come on again... There's no point in living! What's the good of it all, what's the good if it's only to bring us to this? Stop it, you must stop it, Superintendent.

ARCHITECT: Easy to say.

BÉRENGER: I suppose you *are* the police superintendent of the district too?

ARCHITECT: As a matter of fact, that is also one of my duties. It always is for special architects like me.

BÉRENGER: You're really hoping to arrest him before you retire?

ARCHITECT: [coldly annoyed] Naturally, we're doing all we can!... Look out, not that way, you'll get lost, you're always going round in circles, going back in your own tracks.

BÉRENGER: [pointing quite close to him] Ooh! Is that still the same pool?

ARCHITECT: One's enough for him.

BÉRENGER: Are those the same bodies as just now?

ARCHITECT: Three a day is a fair average, what more do you want?

BÉRENGER: Show me the way!... Let's go!...

ARCHITECT: [taking him by the arm and guiding him] This way.

BÉRENGER: And the day started so well! I shall always see those people drowned, I shall always have that picture in my mind.

ARCHITECT: That's what comes of being so emotional!

BÉRENGER: Never mind, it's better to know it all, better to know it all!...

[*The lighting changes. Now it is grey, and there are faint sounds of the street and the trams.*]

ARCHITECT: Here we are! We're not in the radiant city any more, we've gone through the gates. [*He lets go of* BÉRENGER's *arm.*] We're on the outer boulevard. You see, over there? There's your tram. That's the stop.

BÉRENGER: Where?

ARCHITECT: There, where those people are waiting. It's the terminus. The tram starts off in the opposite direction and takes you straight to the other end of the town, takes you home!

[*You can just see, in perspective, some streets beneath a rainy sky, a few outlines and vague red lights. The designer should see that very gradually everything becomes more real. The change should be brought about by the lighting and with a very small number of props: shop-signs, and advertisements should slowly appear one after the other, but not more than three or four in all.*]

BÉRENGER: I'm frozen.

ARCHITECT: You *are*. You're shivering.

BÉRENGER: It's the shock.

ARCHITECT: It's the cold, too. [*He stretches out his hand to feel the raindrops.*] It's raining. Half sleet, half snow.

[BÉRENGER *nearly slips over.*]

Be careful, it's slippery, the pavement's wet. [*He holds him up.*]

BÉRENGER: Thank you.

ARCHITECT: Put your overcoat on or you'll catch cold.

BÉRENGER: Thank you. [*He puts his overcoat on and feverishly ties his scarf round his neck.*] Brr. Goodbye, Monsieur Super-intendent!

ARCHITECT: You're not going straight back home! No one's expecting you... You've plenty of time to have a drink. Do you good. Go on, let yourself go, it's time for that drink before dinner. There's a bistro over there, near the tram-stop, just by the cemetery. They sell wreaths too.

BÉRENGER: You seem to be in a good mood again. I'm not.

ARCHITECT: I was never in a bad one.

BÉRENGER: In spite of...

ARCHITECT: [*interrupting him, as the sign of the bistro lights up*] Have to look life in the face, you know! [*He lays his hand on the handle of an imaginary door, beneath the sign of the bistro.*] Let's go in.

BÉRENGER: I don't feel much like it...

ARCHITECT: Go on in.

BÉRENGER: After you, Monsieur Superintendent.

ARCHITECT: No please, after you.

[*He pushes him. Noise of the bistro door. They come into the shop : this may be the same corner of the stage where the imaginary greenhouse and then the* ARCHITECT'*s imaginary office was before. They go and sit down on two chairs by the little table. They are doubtless next to the big windows of the shop. In the event of the table and chairs having been removed previously, a folding table can be brought on by the* OWNER OF THE BISTRO *when he appears. Two folding chairs could also be picked up from the floor of the stage by* BÉRENGER *and the* ARCHITECT].

Sit down, sit down. [*They sit down.*] You *do* look cheerful! Don't take it to heart so! If we thought about all the misfortunes of mankind we could never go on living. And we must live! All the time there are children with their throats cut, old men starving, mournful widows, orphan girls, people dying, justice miscarrying, houses collapsing on the tenants... mountains crumbling away... massacres, and floods, and dogs run over... That's how journalists earn their daily bread. Everything has it's bright side. In the end it's the bright side you've got to bear in mind.

BÉRENGER: Yes, Monsieur Superintendent, yes... but having been so close and seen with my own eyes... I can't remain indifferent. *You* may have got used to it, you with your two professions.

ARCHITECT: [*slapping* BÉRENGER *on the shoulder*] You're too impressionable, I've told you before. Got to face facts. Come on now, pull yourself together, where's your will-power! [*He slaps him on the shoulder again.* BÉRENGER *nearly falls off the chair.*] You seem fit enough, whatever you say, although you look so sorry for yourself. You're healthy in mind and body!

BÉRENGER: I don't say I'm not. What I'm suffering from doesn't show, it's theoretical, spiritual.

ARCHITECT: I see.

BÉRENGER: You're being sarcastic.

ARCHITECT: I wouldn't dream of it. I've seen quite a few cases like yours among my patients.

BÉRENGER: Yes, of course, you're a doctor too.

ARCHITECT: When I've a minute to spare, I do a little general medicine, I took over from a psychoanalyst and was assistant to a surgeon in my youth, I've also studied sociology... Come on now, let's try and cheer you up. [*Clapping his hands.*] Monsieur!

BÉRENGER: I'm not as versatile as you.

[*From the wings on the left can be heard the voice of a* CLOCHARD.]

CLOCHARD: [*off*] When I left the Merchant Navy
I got spliced to young Octavie!

VOICE OF OWNER: [*loud voice*] Be right with you, Monsieur Superintendent! [*Change of tone; still in the wings to the* CLOCHARD:]
Get out of here, go and get drunk somewhere else!

CLOCHARD: [*off. Thick voice*] What's the point? I'm drunk already!

[*The drunken* CLOCHARD *appears from the left, brutally pushed on stage by the* OWNER, *a dark fat character with great hairy arms.*]
I got drunk at your place, paid for it, shouldn't have given me the stuff!

OWNER: I told you to get out! [*To* ARCHITECT:] Glad to see you, Monsieur Superintendent.

ARCHITECT: [*to* BÉRENGER] You see... We aren't in the beautiful district any more, people's manners aren't so good to start with.

CLOCHARD: [*still being pushed by the* OWNER] What you up to?

BÉRENGER: [*to* ARCHITECT] So I see!

OWNER: [*to* CLOCHARD] Off you go... Look, the Superintendent's over there!

CLOCHARD: Not doing anyone any harm! [*While still being pushed he stumbles and falls full length, but picks himself up without protest.*]

ARCHITECT: [*to* OWNER] Two Beaujolais.

OWNER: Right, sir. I've got some of the real stuff for you. [*To the* CLOCHARD, *who is getting up:*] Get out and close the door behind you, don't let me catch you again. [*He goes off left.*]

ARCHITECT: [*to* BÉRENGER] Still feeling depressed?

BÉRENGER: [*with a helpless gesture to the empty air*] What do you expect!

[*The* OWNER *appears with two glasses of wine, while the* CLOCHARD *closes the door in mime and leaves the shop.*]

OWNER: Your Beaujolais, Monsieur Superintendent!

CLOCHARD: [*going off right, still staggering and singing*]:
When I left the Merchant Navy
I got spliced to young Octavie!

OWNER: [*to* ARCHITECT] You want a snack, Monsieur Superintendent?

ARCHITECT: Give us a couple of sandwiches.

OWNER: I've got a first-class rabbit pâté, pure pork!

[BÉRENGER *shows signs of wanting to pay.*]

ARCHITECT: [*laying his hand on* BÉRENGER'*s arm, to stop him*] No, no, not you! This is on me! [*To* OWNER:] This is on me!

OWNER: Right, Monsieur Superintendent! [*He goes off left. The* ARCHITECT *takes a sip of the wine.* BÉRENGER *does not touch his.*]

BÉRENGER: [*after a short pause*] If only you had a description of him.

ARCHITECT: But we have. At least we know how he looks to his victims. Pictures of him have been stuck on all the walls. We've done our best.

BÉRENGER: How did you get them?

ARCHITECT: They were found on the bodies of the drowned. Some of the people have been brought back to life for a moment and they even provided other information. We know how he sets about it too. So does everyone in the district.

BÉRENGER: But why aren't they more careful? They only have to avoid him.

ARCHITECT: It's not so simple. I tell you, every evening there are always two or three who fall into the trap. But *he* never gets caught.

BÉRENGER: It's beyond me.

[*The* ARCHITECT *takes another sip of wine. The* OWNER *brings the two sandwiches and goes out.*]

I'm amazed... but you, Monsieur Superintendent, seem almost amused by the whole business.

ARCHITECT: I can't help it. After all, it is quite interesting. You see, it's there... Look through the window. [*He pretends to be pulling an imaginary curtain aside; or perhaps a real curtain could have appeared; he points to the left:*] You see... it's there, at the tram-stop, he strikes. When the people get off to go home, they walk to the gates, because they're not allowed to use their private cars outside the radiant city, and that's when he comes to meet them, disguised as a beggar. He starts whining, as they all do, asks for alms and tries to rouse their pity. The usual thing: just out of hospital, no work, looking for a job, nowhere to spend the night. That's not what does the trick, that's only a start. He's feeling his way, he chooses a likely prey, gets into converstation, hangs on and won't be shaken off. He offers to sell a few small articles he takes from his basket, artificial flowers, birds, old-style nightcaps, maps... postcards... American cigarettes, obscene little drawings, all sorts of objects. Generally his offerings are refused, his client hurries on, no time to spare. Still haggling, they both arrive at the pool you already know. Then, suddenly, the big moment arrives; he suggests showing the Colonel's photo. This is irresistible.

As it's getting rather dark, the client leans forward to get a
better view. But now it's too late. A close scrutiny of the
picture is a disturbing experience. Taking advantage of this he
gives a push and the victim falls in the pool and is drowned.
The blow is struck, all he has to do now is to look for fresh
prey.

BÉRENGER: What's so extraordinary is that people know and still
let themselves be taken in.

ARCHITECT: That's the trick, you know. He's never been caught
in the act.

BÉRENGER: Incredible! Incredible!

ARCHITECT: And yet it's true! [*He bites into his sandwich.*] You're
not drinking? Or eating?

> [*Noise of a tram arriving at the stop.* BÉRENGER *instinctively
> raises his head quickly and goes to pull the curtain aside to look
> through the window in the direction of the tram-stop.*]

That's the tram arriving.

BÉRENGER: Groups of people are getting out!

ARCHITECT: Of course. The people who live in the district.
Going home.

BÉRENGER: I can't see any beggars.

ARCHITECT: You won't. He'll not show himself. He knows
we're here.

BÉRENGER: [*turning his back to the window and coming back to the*
ARCHITECT, *who also has his back to the window, to sit down again*]
Perhaps it would be a good idea if you had a plainclothes in-
spector permanently on duty at this spot.

ARCHITECT: You want to teach me how to do my job? Technic-
ally, it's not possible. Our inspectors are overworked, they've
got other things to do. Besides, *they'd* want to see the Colonel's
photo too. There have been five of them drowned already like
that. Ah... If we could prove his identity, we'd know where to
find him!

> [*Suddenly a cry is heard, and the heavy sound of a body falling into
> water.*]

BÉRENGER: [*jumping to his feet*] Did you hear that?

ARCHITECT: [*still seated, biting his sandwich*] He's struck again. You see how easy it is to stop him. As soon as your back's turned, a second's inattention, and there you are... One second, that's all he needs.

BÉRENGER: It's terrible, terrible!

[*Muttering voices are heard, alarmed voices coming from the wings, the sound of footsteps, and a police car's screaming brakes.*] [*Wringing his hands:*] Do something, do *something*... Intervene, move!...

ARCHITECT: [*calmly, still sitting, sandwich in hand, after another sip*] It's far too late now. Once again, he's taken us unawares...

BÉRENGER: Perhaps it's just a big stone he's thrown in the water... to tease us!

ARCHITECT: That *would* surprise me. And the cry?

[*The* OWNER *comes in from the left.*]

Now we'll know everything, anyway. Here comes our informer.

OWNER: It's the girl, the blonde one...

BÉRENGER: Dany? Mademoiselle Dany? It can't be!

ARCHITECT: It is. Why not? She's my secretary, my ex-secretary. And I gave her fair warning not to leave my staff. She was safe there.

BÉRENGER: Oh God, God, God!

ARCHITECT: She was in the Civil Service! He doesn't attack the Service! But no, she wanted her 'liberty'! That'll teach her. She's found it now, her liberty. I was expecting this...

BÉRENGER: Oh God, oh God! Poor girl... She didn't have time to say Yes to me!

ARCHITECT: [*continuing*] I was even sure it would happen! Unless she'd gone right out of the district as soon as she left the Service.

BÉRENGER: Mademoiselle Dany! Mademoiselle Dany! Mademoiselle Dany! [*Lamentation*]

ARCHITECT: [*continuing*] Ah! People are so determined to have their own way, and above all the victims are so determined to revisit the scene of the crime! That's how they get caught!

BÉRENGER: [*almost sobbing*] Ooh! Monsieur Superintendent. Monsieur Superintendent, it's Mademoiselle Dany, Mademoiselle Dany! [*He crumples up on his chair, in a state of collapse.*]

ARCHITECT: [*to* OWNER] Make the usual report, routine, you know. [*He takes his telephone from his pocket:*] Hullo?... Hullo?... Another one... It's a young woman... Dany... the one who worked with us... No one caught in the act... Just suspicions... the same ones... yes!... One moment! [*He lays the telephone on the table.*]

BÉRENGER: [*suddenly jumps to his feet*] We can't, we mustn't let things go on like this! It's got to stop! It's got to stop!

ARCHITECT: Control yourself. We've all got to die. Let the investigation take its usual course!

BÉRENGER: [*runs off, slamming the imaginary shop-door with a bang, which is however heard*] It can't go on! We must *do* something! We must, we must, we must! [*He goes off right.*]

OWNER: Au revoir, Monsieur! [*To* ARCHITECT:] He might say goodbye!

ARCHITECT: [*still seated, he watches him go, like the* OWNER, *who is standing with his arms folded or his hands on his hips; then, as soon as* BÉRENGER *has gone, the* ARCHITECT *tosses off the rest of his wine and pointing to* BÉRENGER's *full glass says to the* OWNER] Drink it! Eat the sandwich too!

[*The* OWNER *sits down in* BÉRENGER's *place. On the telephone:*] Hullo! No evidence! Close the case! Crime unsolved! [*He puts the telephone back in his pocket.*]

OWNER: [*drinking*] Santé! [*He bites into the sandwich.*]

CURTAIN

ACT TWO

BÉRENGER's *room. Dark and low-ceilinged, but lighter in the*

*centre opposite the window. Near this long low window a chest.
To the right of it a gloomy recess; in this dark patch an armchair,
French Regency style, rather knocked about, in which, as the
curtain rises, ÉDOUARD is sitting, silently. At the beginning of the
Act he is not visible, nor is the armchair, because of the darkness
that reigns in BÉRENGER's ground-floor room.*

*In the centre, in the brightest part, a large table in front of the
window, with notebooks and papers, a book, an inkstand and
a fancy penholder like a goose-quill.*

*A red worn-out armchair with one arm missing is a few feet to the
left of the table. In the left hand wall, more shadowy corners.*

*In the rest of the room you can make out in the half-light the
shapes of old pieces of furniture: an old writing-desk and a chest
of drawers with a threadbare tapestry on the wall above it; there
is also a chair and another red armchair. Next to the window, on
the right, a small table, a footstool and some shelves with a few
books. On the top an old gramophone.*

*At the front of the stage on the left is the door that gives on the
landing. Hanging from the ceiling an old chandelier: on the floor a
faded old carpet. On the right hand wall a mirror in a baroque
frame, which shines so little at the beginning of the act that it is
difficult to tell what the object is. Beneath the mirror an old
chimney-piece.*

*The curtains are not drawn, and through the window you can see
the street, the windows of the ground floor opposite and a part of
the front of a grocer's shop.*

*The decor of Act II is very much constructed, heavy, realistic and
ugly; it contrasts strongly with the lack of decor and the simple
lighting effects of Act I.*

*When the curtain rises the window lights the middle of the stage
and the central table with a pale yellowish light. The walls of the
house opposite are a dirty grey colour. Outside the weather is dull;
it is half snowing, half drizzling.*

*Sitting in the armchair in the darkest corner of BÉRENGER's room,
to the right of the window, ÉDOUARD is neither seen nor heard at*

the start of the Act. He will be seen later, after BÉRENGER's *arrival : thin, very pale, feverish-looking, dressed in black, with a mourning band round his right arm, a black felt hat, black over-coat, black shoes, white shirt with starched collar and black tie. Now and again, but only after* BÉRENGER's *arrival,* ÉDOUARD *will cough or clear his throat ; from time to time he spits into a great white handkerchief with a black border, which he fastidiously returns to his pocket.*

A few moments before the rise of the curtain the VOICE OF THE CONCIERGE *is already heard coming from the left, that is from the landing in the block of flats.*

CONCIERGE: [*singing*] When it's cold it's not hot,
　　　　　　　　　When it's hot, it's because it's cold!
Oh dear, you can sweep as much as you like, it's dirty all day long, what with their snow and their coal dust.

[*Noise of a broom knocking against the door, then the* CONCIERGE *is heard singing again :*]

　　　When it's cold it's not hot,
　　　When it's hot it's because it's cold,
　　　When it's cold, it can't be hot!
　　　When it's hot, how can it be cold?
　　　What *is* it then when it's cold?
　　　Cold as cold, and that's your lot!

[*During the song of the* CONCIERGE *there are sounds of ham-mering from the floor above, a radio blaring and trucks and motorcycles approaching and dying away ; at one point too the shouts of children in the schoolyard during recreation : all this must be slightly distorted, caricatured, so the cries of the schoolchildren sound like dogs yapping ; the idea is to make the uproar sound worse, but in a way that is partly unpleasant and partly comic.*]

MAN'S VOICE: [*preceded by the noise of footsteps on the stairs and the barking of a dog*] Good morning, Madame la Concierge.

VOICE OF CONCIERGE: Good morning, Monsieur Lelard! You're late leaving this morning!

MAN'S VOICE: I've had some work to do at home. I've been asleep. Feel better now. Going to post my letters.

VOICE OF CONCIERGE: You've a funny sort of job! Always working with papers! Writing all those letters, you must have to think all the time.

MAN'S VOICE: It's not writing them that makes me think, but sending them off.

VOICE OF CONCIERGE: Yes, you've got to know who to send them to! Can't send them to *anyone!* Mustn't send them all to the same person, eh?

MAN'S VOICE: Still, got to earn your living by the sweat of your brow, as the prophet says.

VOICE OF CONCIERGE: There's too much education these days, that's where things go wrong. Take sweeping, even that's not as easy as it used to be.

MAN'S VOICE: Still, got to earn your living anyway, to pay your income tax.

VOICE OF CONCIERGE: Minister in Parliament, that's the best job. They don't *pay* taxes, they *collect* them.

MAN'S VOICE: Even poor chaps like them have to earn their living, just like anyone else.

VOICE OF CONCIERGE: Yes, the rich are probably as poor as us, if there's any left these days.

MAN'S VOICE: Ah yes, that's life.

VOICE OF CONCIERGE: Ah yes, afraid so!

MAN'S VOICE: Ah yes, Madame.

VOICE OF CONCIERGE: Ah yes, Monsieur. It's a dog's life, and we all end up in the same place, a hole in the ground. That's where my husband is, forty years ago he died, and it's just like yesterday. [*A dog barks at the entrance.*] Shut up, Treasure. [*She must have clouted the dog with her broom, for you can hear his plaintive yelps. A door bangs.*] Go back in. [*To the* MAN *presumably:*] Oh well, goodbye Monsieur Lelard. Careful now, it's slippery outside, the pavements are all wet. Stinking weather!

MAN'S VOICE: I'll say it is. We were talking about life, Madame, we've got to be philosophical, you know!

VOICE OF CONCIERGE: Don't you talk to me about philosophers! I once got it into my head to be all stoical and go in for meditation. They never taught me anything, even that Marcus Aurelius. Doesn't really do any good. We know as much as he does. We all have to find our own way out. If there was one, but there isn't.

MAN'S VOICE: Ah yes!...

VOICE OF CONCIERGE: And do without feelings too, how are we meant to find room for them? They don't enter into our account of things. How would feelings help *me* sweep my staircase?

MAN'S VOICE: I haven't read the philosophers.

VOICE OF CONCIERGE: You haven't missed much. That's what comes of being educated like you. Philosophy's no good, except to put in a test-tube. May turn it a pretty colour, if you're lucky!

MAN'S VOICE: You shouldn't say that.

VOICE OF CONCIERGE: Philosophers! They're no good, except for a concierge like me.

MAN'S VOICE: You shouldn't say that, Madame, they're good for everyone.

VOICE OF CONCIERGE: I know what I'm talking about. You, you only read *good* books. I read the *philosophers*, because I've no money, the twopenny halfpenny philosophers. You, even if you've no money either, at least you can go to a library. You've got books to *choose* from... and what's the good of it, I ask you, you ought to know.

MAN'S VOICE: Philosophy, I say, is good for learning a philosophy of life!

VOICE OF CONCIERGE: I know all about the philosophy of life.

MAN'S VOICE: Good for you, Madame!

[*The broom knocks against the bottom of the door of* BÉRENGER'*s room.*]

VOICE OF CONCIERGE: Oh dear, oh dear, what a dirty house this is! It's the slush!

MAN'S VOICE: Plenty of that about. Oh well, I'm off this time, time's pressing on. Au revoir, Madame, keep smiling.

VOICE OF CONCIERGE: Thanks, Monsieur Lelard! [*The entrance door is banged violently.*] Oh, that's clever of him, silly fool will smash the door next, and *I'll* have to pay for it!

MAN'S VOICE: [*politely*] Did you say something, Madame?

VOICE OF CONCIERGE: [*more politely still, sweetly*] It's nothing, Monsieur Lelard, just chatting to myself, learning to talk! Makes the time go quicker!

[*The broom knocks against the bottom of the door of* BÉRENGER's *room.*]

MAN'S VOICE: I quite thought you'd called me. Sorry.

VOICE OF CONCIERGE: Oh well, we all make mistakes, you know, Monsieur! Can't help it! No harm done. [*The front door is slammed violently again.*] He's gone this time. Tell him the same thing over and over again, he doesn't listen, him and his doors. Anybody'd think he was deaf! Likes to pretend he is, but he can hear all right! [*She sings:*]
When it's cold, it's not hot.
[*Yapping of the dog, more muffled.*] Shut up, Treasure! Ah, call that a dog! You wait, I'll knock hell out of you! [*You can hear the door of the* CONCIERGE's *room opening. The dog yelps. The same door bangs again.*]

ANOTHER MAN'S VOICE: [*after the sound of footsteps: slightly foreign accent*] Good morning, Madame la Concierge! Mademoiselle Colombine, she live here?

VOICE OF CONCIERGE: Can't say I know the name! There aren't any foreigners in the house. Only French people.

SECOND MAN: [*at the same time the upstairs radio is turned up very loud*] But they told me she live on fifth floor this block.

VOICE OF CONCIERGE: [*shouting to make herself heard*] Can't say I know the name, I tell you!

SECOND MAN'S VOICE: Please, Madame? [*Coming from the street on the right, the lumbering sound of a truck, which suddenly brakes a few seconds later.*]

VOICE OF CONCIERGE: [*still shouting*] I tell you I don't know the name!

SECOND MAN'S VOICE: This Number Thirteen, Twelfth Street?

VOICE OF CONCIERGE: [*as before*] What Street?

SECOND MAN'S VOICE: [*louder*] This Number Thirteen...

VOICE OF CONCIERGE: [*yelling*] Don't shout so loud. I can hear you. Of course it's Number Thirteen, Twelfth Street. Can't you read? It's written up outside.

SECOND MAN'S VOICE: Then it must be here Mademoiselle Colombine lives!

TRUCK DRIVER VOICE: [*in the street*] Goddam learn to drive!

VOICE OF CONCIERGE: I know better than you.

CAR DRIVER'S VOICE: [*in the street*] Don't you goddam me!

VOICE OF CONCIERGE: Oh, I see, Mademoiselle Colombine, perhaps you mean Monsieur Lecher's concubine?

TRUCK DRIVER'S VOICE: [*in the street*] Bastard! Pimp!

SECOND MAN'S VOICE: Yes, that's it! Latcher!

VOICE OF CONCIERGE: Latcher, Lecher, it's all the same!

CAR DRIVER: [*in the street*] Can't you be polite, damn you?

VOICE OF CONCIERGE: So it's the redhead you're after! If she's the one, *she* lives here, I told you she did! You want to say what you mean! Take the elevator!

TRUCK DRIVER: [*in the street*] Son of a bitch!

CAR DRIVER: [*in the street*] Son of a bitch, yourself. [*Combined noises of the elevator going up, the radio, vehicles starting up again in the street, and then the splutter of a motorbike; for a split second you can see the motorcyclist through the window, passing in the street.*]

VOICE OF CONCIERGE: [*loudly*] Don't forget to shut the elevator door after you! [*To herself:*] They always forget, especially foreigners! [*She sings:*]

Of course you never get on, if you stay in the same places,
But do you really get on, if you're always changing places?

[*The door of the* CONCIERGE's *flat is heard banging ; she has gone in :
the dog yaps, her voice is more muffled :*] Yes, come on, my little
Treasure! Who hasn't had his lump of sugar? Here it is, here's
your sugar for you! [*Yapping*] Take that! [*The dog howls. In
the street two people can be seen through the window, coming on
from the left. Or possibly you just hear them talking, without seeing
them. Two* OLD MEN, *both decrepit, who hobble along painfully,
taking small steps and leaning on their sticks.*]

1ST O.M.: Terrible weather.

2ND O.M.: Terrible weather.

1ST O.M.: What you say?

2ND O.M.: Terrible weather. What *you* say?

1ST O.M.: I said: terrible weather.

2ND O.M.: Hang on to my arm, you might slip over.

1ST O.M.: Hang on to my arm, you might slip over.

2ND O.M.: I used to know some surprising people, very surprising.

CLOCHARD: [*appearing from the right on the pavement opposite : he is
singing*] When I left the Merchant Navy. [*He looks up at the
windows; some coins could be thrown down.*]

1ST O.M.: What did they do, these surprising people?

2ND O.M.: They surprised everyone!

CLOCHARD: I got spliced to young Octavie!

1ST O.M.: And where did these surprising people surprise?

[*The* CLOCHARD *does as before.*]

2ND O.M.: They surprised in society circles... everywhere they
surprised!

1ST O.M.: When did you know them, these surprising people?

CLOCHARD: [*as before*] When I left the Merchant Navy...
[*Still looking up at the windows of the upper floors, he makes off
left and disappears.*]

2ND O.M.: In the old days, the old days...

1ST O.M.: Do you still see them sometimes?

GROCER: [*coming out of the shop opposite, looking furious and gazing
up at a first-floor window*] Hey Madame!

2ND O.M.: Ah, my dear chap, there aren't any more nowadays, there aren't any more people who surprise... [*He is seen disappearing on the right, and you can hear:*] All that's gone. I only know two of them today... two surprising people...

GROCER: Hey Madame! Who do you take me for?

2ND O.M.: ...only two. One of them's retired and the other's deceased. [*The* IST OLD MAN *disappears too.*]

GROCER: [*as before*] I mean... who do you take me for?

VOICE OF CLOCHARD: [*singing*] The Captain of the tanker.

GROCER: [*as before*] Who do you take me for? I'm a shopkeeper, Madame, not a ragman! [*He goes furiously back to his shop.*]

VOICE OF CLOCHARD: [*moving away*]
    Sent for me and said
    If you want to get spliced to young Octavie
    You'd better leave the Merchant Navy...

VOICE OF IST O.M.: [*moving away*] If there were any, you wouldn't notice. Surprising people don't surprise any more.

[*From the right the noise of recreation, which has already been heard quietly, redoubles in intensity. A schoolbell rings.*]

SCHOOLMASTER VOICE: Back to class! Back to class!

VOICE FROM THE STREET: We've fifty-eight delivery boys...

SCHOOLMASTER VOICE: Silence! [*Stamping of feet, shouting, noise of desks, etc. from the right.*] Silence! Silence!

VOICE FROM THE STREET: We've fifty-eight delivery boys!

[*The children in the school are silent.*]

SCHOOLMASTER VOICE: History lesson: the people's representatives came to the gates of the palace of Queen Marie Antoinette. And they shouted...

VOICE FROM THE STREET: We've fifty-eight delivery boys!

SCHOOLMASTER VOICE: They shouted: we haven't any more cake, Your Majesty, give us cake. There isn't any left, replied the Queen.

VOICE FROM THE STREET: We've fifty-eight delivery boys!

SCHOOLMASTER VOICE: There isn't any left, why don't you eat bread? Then the people grew angry and cut off the Queen's head. When the Queen saw that she'd lost her head, she was so upset she had a stroke. She couldn't get over it, whatever the doctors did. They weren't up to much at the time.

VOICE FROM THE STREET: We've fifty-eight delivery boys!

GRUFF VOICE: [*in the street*] We were seven thousand feet up, when suddenly I saw the wing of our plane coming off.

ANOTHER VOICE: [*thin and piping*] You don't say!

GRUFF VOICE: All right, I said to myself, we've still got one left. The passengers all piled up on one side of the plane to keep an even keel and it went flying on with one wing.

PIPING VOICE: Were you frightened?

GRUFF VOICE: You wait... suddenly the second wing fell off, and then the engines... and the propellers... and we were seven thousand feet up!

PIPING VOICE: Phew!

GRUFF VOICE: This time I thought we'd had it... [*The voice fades:*] Really had it, no way out... Well, do you know what saved us? Give you three guesses...

VOICE FROM THE STREET: Our fifty-eight delivery boys waste too much time urinating. Five times a day, on average, they interrupt their deliveries to satisfy a personal need. The time is not deducted from their wages. They take advantage of this, so they've got to be disciplined; they can make water in turn once a month for four and a half hours without interruption. That will save all the coming and going, which sends up our costs. After all, *camels* store up water.

IST VOICE FROM BELOW: I went to catch my train, find my compartment and sit down in my reserved seat. The train was about to leave. Just at that minute in comes a gentlemen with the same seat and the same number as me. Out of politeness I gave my seat up and went and stood in the corridor. He hardly said thank you. I stood for two hours. In the end the train stopped at a station and the man got off. I went and sat down again, as the seat was mine in the first place. Again the train pulled out. An hour later it stopped at another station. And the

same man gets in again and wants his seat back! Legally had
he any right to it? It was my seat as well as his, but he claimed
second occupant's rights. We went to law about it. The judge
said the man was entitled to extra privileges, because he was a
blue-blooded critic*, and it was only modesty made him con-
ceal his identity.

ANOTHER VOICE FROM BELOW: Who was the gentleman?

1ST VOICE: A national hero. Harold Hastings de Hobson.*

2ND VOICE: How did he manage to catch the same train again?

1ST VOICE: He took a short cutting.

VOICE FROM THE STREET: [closer] We've fifty-eight delivery boys.

[The two OLD MEN reappear in the street from the opposite
direction, that is from the left.]

1ST O.M.: I was invited to the wedding reception, of course...
I wasn't very satisfied because all I like is coq au vin...

2ND O.M.: They didn't serve any coq au vin?

1ST O.M.: They did. But they didn't tell me it was coq au vin, so
it didn't taste right.

2ND O.M.: Was it really coq au vin?

1ST O.M.: It WAS coq au vin, but as I didn't know, the whole
meal was a farce.

2ND O.M.: I wish I'd been invited instead of you. I like my
dishes farcis. [They go off.]

VOICE FROM THE STREET: We've fifty-eight delivery boys!

VOICE FROM RIGHT: We must seriously raise the question of our
finances.

VOICE FROM ABOVE: Has the problem been considered by the
delegation of deputy delegates?

VOICE FROM LEFT: We must seriously raise the question of their
finances.

VOICE FROM ABOVE: We must seriously raise the question of the

---

* There is a pun here in the original on the name of the French writer and dramatic critic, Morvan Lebesque. Harold Hobson is a natural choice in England for
his well known admiration of French drama. American readers might like to pun
on the name of an American critic. Tr.

finances of our delivery boys.

ANOTHER VOICE FROM LEFT: No, the problem's been solved by the delegate of the deputy delegation.

VOICE FROM RIGHT: After all, production is production! The whole basis of the problem must be re-examined.

VOICE FROM LEFT: With our overseers and our underseers, our visionaries and our viewfinders, we shall form an organizational basis, a common funds committee.

VOICE FROM ABOVE: The seers and the underseers will form development committees for companies of contractors who will form special communities. . .

VOICE FROM RIGHT: There's the basic organizational principle and the organizational aspect of the superstructure.

VOICE FROM LEFT: What about our fifty-eight delivery boys?

VOICE FROM ABOVE: After work, we must organize leisure.

VOICE FROM BELOW: Concentrated leisure.

VOICE FROM LEFT: We must force the pace of leisure.

[*For some seconds thick fog darkens the stage: for a while the sounds from outside are muffled, all you can hear are vague snatches of dialogue.*]

VOICE OF CONCIERGE: [*after a banging of doors in the entrance*] Oh, when the fog's mixed with the factory smoke, you can't hear a word! [*Strident whistle from a factory hooter.*] Thank God for the hooters!

[*The fog has lifted, and on the other side of the street, you can see the* CLOCHARD *singing:*]

CLOCHARD: The second in command
　　　　　Sent for me and told me
　　　　　To marry my Octavie
　　　　　To marry my Octavie

[*The street sounds fade a little to facilitate the following scene.*]
　　　　　And I'd be as good a slavey
　　　　　As I'd once been in the Navy!

[*In the entrance a door is heard banging, while the* CLOCHARD, *still singing, looks up at the windows to catch the coins as they fall, takes off his battered old hat in general acknowledgment and comes nearer the window, advancing into the middle of the street.*]

VOICE OF CONCIERGE: Don't bang the door like that!

WOMAN'S VOICE: [*in the entrance*] You bang it too sometimes. I didn't mean to.

VOICE OF CONCIERGE: Yes, but with me it's because I don't know when I'm doing it.

CLOCHARD: [*in the street, looking up at the windows*] Thank you, ladies and gentlemen, thank you! [*He starts muttering when there are no coins falling.*] They're a stingy lot, curse 'em!

VOICE OF CONCIERGE: [*singing*] Cold as cold
                              And that's your lot.

CLOCHARD: [*while the* CONCIERGE *goes on singing the same refrain, he has crossed the street. A motorcyclist brushes past him from behind, travelling fast, and a voice is heard: 'Stupid bastard'*] As I'd once been in the Navy! [*He is right up to the window, and as he sings:*

But keep a weather eye,
But keep a weather eye!...

he looks through the window into BÉRENGER'*s room, squashing his face and nose up against the glass.*]

CONCIERGE: [*making her appearance on the pavement, which she is sweeping, singing away until she bumps into the* CLOCHARD] What are you doing here?

CLOCHARD: I'm singing!

CONCIERGE: You're dirtying the window panes! That's one of my tenants, and I'm the one has to keep them clean.

CLOCHARD: [*sarcastically*] Oh! I beg your pardon, Madame. I didn't know. No need to get upset.

CONCIERGE: Go on, clear off and don't be a nuisance!

CLOCHARD: [*still a bit cheeky and rather drunk*] I've heard that a thousand times before. You're not very original, Madame.

CONCIERGE: [*threatening him with her broom*] I'll teach you to play the critic with me.

CLOCHARD: Don't trouble yourself, Madame, I'm going, Ma-

dame, I'm sorry! [*He moves off, still singing :*]
   When I left the Merchant Navy
   I got spliced to young Octavie.
CONCIERGE: [*still in the street near the window, she wheels round as
   the dog barks*] Shut up!... The postman! [*To the* POSTMAN:]
   Who's it for, Postman?
POSTMAN'S VOICE: Telegram for Monsieur Bérenger!
CONCIERGE: Ground floor, on the right.
POSTMAN'S VOICE: Thanks.
CONCIERGE: [*waving her broom after the* CLOCHARD, *who is no
   longer visible*] Lazy old bugger! [*Shrugging her shoulders :*]
   If he's a sailor, I'm a tart!
      [*The* POSTMAN *is heard knocking at* BÉRENGER'S *door, while the*
      CONCIERGE *sweeps the pavement.*]
   Oh, all this dog's mess, I wouldn't let mine do it.
POSTMAN'S VOICE: No reply.
CONCIERGE: [*to invisible* POSTMAN] Knock louder. He's there.
POSTMAN'S VOICE: I tell you there's no reply.
CONCIERGE: Don't even know how to knock on a door! [*She dis-
   appears into the entrance.*] Of course he can't have gone out. I
   ought to know his habits. He is my tenant. I even do his house-
   work. Clean his windows!
POSTMAN'S VOICE: Try!
      [*Loud knocking is heard, repeated several times, on* BÉRENGER'S
      door.]
VOICE OF CONCIERGE: [*knocking at the door*] Monsieur Bérenger!
   Monsieur Bérenger! [*Silence, then more knocking.*] Monsieur
   Bérenger! Monsieur Bérenger!
POSTMAN'S VOICE: What did I tell you!
VOICE OF CONCIERGE: Well, I like that! He can't have gone out.
   Could be asleep, but that's not one of his habits! Knock
   louder! I'll go and look!
      [*The* POSTMAN *goes on knocking and the* CONCIERGE *appears
      again outside the window ; she glues her face to the window pane.
      Her face is naturally hideous, but with her nose squashed against*

the glass it looks even worse.]

CONCIERGE: Monsieur Bérenger! I say, Monsieur Bérenger!

[*At the same time the* POSTMAN *is heard knocking at the door.*]

POSTMAN'S VOICE: Monsieur Bérenger! Telegram, Monsieur Bérenger!

CONCIERGE: Monsieur Bérenger, there's a telegram for you... fine state of affairs! [*Pause*] Where on earth can he be? He's never at home! [*She raps on the window again, while the* POST-MAN'S *knocking continues.*] Some people go for walks, got nothing better to do, and we work our fingers to the bone!... He's not there! [*She disappears: she must be near the entrance as you can see her arm brandishing the broom out of one corner of the window.*]

POSTMAN'S VOICE: If he's not in, he's not in. And you said he never went out!

VOICE OF CONCIERGE: I didn't! Give me the telegram, I'll give it to him! [*She disappears completely.*] I'm the one cleans his windows!

POSTMAN'S VOICE: I'm not allowed to give it to you. I can't.

VOICE OF CONCIERGE: That's that, then, keep it.

POSTMAN'S VOICE: I'll give it you anyway. Here it is.

CONCIERGE: Now I've got to keep a look-out for him! Oh dear!

[*Pause. The noises have suddenly ceased, after the dying fall of one last factory siren. Perhaps too the* CONCIERGE *has been heard for one last time abusing her dog, which yelps as usual. A few moments' silence. Then, passing along the street close to the window,* BÉRENGER *can be seen coming home. He has his overcoat on and is clutching his hat in his right hand; he is swinging his arm vigorously. He is walking with his head down. Once he has gone past the window his steps are heard in the entrance. Then his key turns in the lock.*]

VOICE OF CONCIERGE: [*very polite*] Why, it's you, Monsieur Bérenger! Had a nice walk? You need some fresh air! Good idea!

VOICE OF BÉRENGER: Good morning, Madame.

VOICE OF CONCIERGE: If you've been for a walk, you must have
gone out. Didn't hear you go. Why didn't you tell me, I
hadn't got a key to do your room. How could I know? *I* was
ready. Telegram came for you.
[*Pause.* BÉRENGER *has stopped opening the door to read the
telegram.*]
I hope it wasn't urgent? I read it, you see. It's the old clothes
man. Wants you, urgently. Nothing to worry about.
[*The key is again heard grating in the lock. The door of* BÉRENGER'*s
room opens quietly. The* CONCIERGE *is heard angrily muttering
words that are indistinguishable, then she bangs the door of her
flat and the dog squeals. The figure of* BÉRENGER *can be picked out
in the dim room. He advances slowly towards the centre of the
stage. The silence is complete. He turns the electric light switch
and the stage lights up.* ÉDOUARD *is seen in his corner, with his
hat on his head, wearing his overcoat, his briefcase at his feet,
clearing his throat. Surprised, first by the coughing, then almost
at the same time by the sight of* ÉDOUARD *himself,* BÉRENGER
gives a jump.*]
BÉRENGER: Oh, what are you doing here?
ÉDOUARD: [*in a thin, rather high-pitched voice, almost childlike, as he
gets up coughing, picking up his briefcase, which he keeps in his
hand*] Your place isn't very warm. [*He spits into his handkerchief.
To do this he has laid his briefcase down again and taken his right
hand out of his pocket; this arm is slightly withered and visibly
shorter than the other. Then, carefully and methodically, he folds
his handkerchief again, puts it back in his pocket and picks up his
briefcase.*]
BÉRENGER: You startled me... I wasn't expecting you, what are
you doing here?
ÉDOUARD: Waiting for you. [*Putting his deformed hand back in his
pocket.*] How are you, Bérenger?
BÉRENGER: How did you get in?
ÉDOUARD: Through the door, of course. I opened it.
BÉRENGER: How? I had the keys with me!

ÉDOUARD: [*taking some keys from his pocket and showing them to* BÉRENGER] So did I! [*He puts the keys back in his pocket.*]

BÉRENGER: How did you get those keys? [*He lays his hat on the table.*]

ÉDOUARD: But... you let me have them for a while yourself, so I could come to your flat when I liked, and wait for you if you were out.

BÉRENGER: [*trying to remember*] I gave you those keys?... When?... I don't remember at all...

ÉDOUARD: You gave them to me all the same. How else could I have got them?

BÉRENGER: Édouard, it's amazing. Still, if you say...

ÉDOUARD: I promise you did... I'm sorry, Bérenger, I'll give them back if you don't want me to have them.

BÉRENGER: Oh... no, no... keep them, Édouard, keep them now you've got them. I'm sorry, I've a bad memory. I don't remember giving them to you.

ÉDOUARD: Well, you did... you remember, it was last year, I think. One Sunday when...

BÉRENGER: [*interrupting him*] The concierge didn't tell me you were waiting.

ÉDOUARD: I don't suppose she saw me, it's my fault, I didn't know I had to ask *her* if I could come to your flat. I thought you told me it wasn't necessary. But if you don't want me here...

BÉRENGER: That's not what I mean. I'm always pleased to see you.

ÉDOUARD: I don't want to be in the way.

BÉRENGER: You know it's not that at all.

ÉDOUARD: Thanks.

BÉRENGER: It's losing my memory that upsets me... [*To himself:*] Still, the concierge oughtn't to have left the flats this morning!... [*To* ÉDOUARD:] What's wrong with you? You're trembling.

ÉDOUARD: Yes, I am. I don't feel very well. I'm cold.

BÉRENGER: [*taking the sound hand in his, while* ÉDOUARD *stuffs the other in his pocket*] You've still got a temperature. Coughing and shivering. You're very pale and your eyes look feverish.

ÉDOUARD: My lungs... they're not improving... after all the time I've had trouble with them...

BÉRENGER: And this building's so badly heated... [*Without taking his overcoat off he goes and sinks morosely into an armchair near the table, while* ÉDOUARD *remains standing.*] Do sit down, Édouard.

ÉDOUARD: Thank you, thanks very much. [*He sits down again on the chest, cautiously setting his briefcase down near him, within reach; he always seems to be keeping an eye on it. A moment's silence. Then, noticing how gloomy* BÉRENGER *is looking and how he is sighing:*] You seem so sad, you look worn out and anxious...

BÉRENGER: [*to himself*] If that was all...

ÉDOUARD: You're not ill too, are you?... What's wrong? Has something happened to you?

BÉRENGER: No, no... nothing at all. I'm like that... I'm not cheerful by nature! Brrr... I'm cold too! [*He rubs his hands.*]

ÉDOUARD: I'm sure something's happened to you. You're more nervous than usual, you're quite jumpy! Tell me about it, if I'm not being indiscreet, it may help.

BÉRENGER: [*getting up and taking a few excited paces in the room*] I've got good reason.

ÉDOUARD: What's wrong?

BÉRENGER: Oh, nothing, nothing and everything... everything...

ÉDOUARD: I should like a cup of tea, if I may...

BÉRENGER: [*suddenly adopting the serious tones of a tragic pronouncement*] My dear Édouard, I am shattered, in despair, inconsolable!

ÉDOUARD: [*without changing the tone of his voice*] Shattered by what, in despair about what?

BÉRENGER: My fiancée has been murdered.

ÉDOUARD: I beg your pardon?

BÉRENGER: My fiancée has been murdered, do you hear?

he not really bereaved
and the other not really consolet
60   IONESCO

ÉDOUARD: Your fiancée? Since when have you been engaged? You never told me you were thinking of getting married. Congratulations. My condolences too. Who was she?

BÉRENGER: To be honest... She wasn't exactly my fiancée... just a girl, a young girl who might have been.

ÉDOUARD: Ah yes?

BÉRENGER: A girl who was as beautiful as she was sweet and tender, pure as an angel. It's terrible. Too terrible.

ÉDOUARD: How long had you known her?

BÉRENGER: Always, perhaps. Since this morning anyway.

ÉDOUARD: Quite recently.

BÉRENGER: She was snatched from me... snatched away!... I... [*Gesture of the hand.*]

ÉDOUARD: It must be very hard... please, have you any tea?

BÉRENGER: I'm sorry, I wasn't thinking... With this tragedy... which has ruined my life! Yes, I've got some.

ÉDOUARD: I understand.

BÉRENGER: You couldn't understand.

ÉDOUARD: Oh yes I do.

BÉRENGER: I can't offer you tea... It's gone mouldy. I'd forgotten.

ÉDOUARD: Well, a glass of rum, please... I'm quite numb with cold...

    [BÉRENGER *produces a bottle of rum, fills a small glass for* ÉDOUARD *and offers it to him while he says:*]

BÉRENGER: No one will ever take her place. My life is over. It's a wound that will never heal.

ÉDOUARD: You really have been wounded, poor old thing! [*Taking the glass of rum.*] Thanks! [*Still in a tone of indifference:*] Poor old thing!

BÉRENGER: And if that was all, if there was nothing but the murder of that unfortunate girl. Do you know the things that happen in the world, awful things, in our town, terrible things, you can't imagine... quite near here... comparatively close... morally speaking it's actually here! [*He strikes his*

breast. ÉDOUARD *has swallowed his rum, chokes and coughs.*]
Aren't you feeling well?

ÉDOUARD: It's nothing. It's so strong. [*He goes on coughing.*] I
must have swallowed it the wrong way.

BÉRENGER: [*gently hitting* ÉDOUARD *on the back to stop him coughing
and with the other hand taking his glass from him*] I thought I'd
found everything again, got it all back. [*To* ÉDOUARD:]
Stretch your head up and look at the ceiling. It'll stop. [*He goes
on :*] All I'd lost and all I hadn't lost, all that had been mine and
all that had never been mine...

ÉDOUARD: [*to* BÉRENGER, *who is still hitting him on the back*] Thank
you... that's enough... you're hurting... stop it, please.

BÉRENGER: [*going to place the little glass on the table while* ÉDOUARD
spits into his handkerchief] I thought the spring had returned for
ever... that I'd found the unfindable again, the dream, the key,
life... all that we've lost while we've gone on living.

ÉDOUARD: [*clearing his throat*] Yes. Of course.

BÉRENGER: All our muddled aspirations, all the things we
vaguely yearn for, from the depths of our being, without even
realizing... Oh, I thought I'd found everything... It was unexplored territory, magically beautiful.

ÉDOUARD: The girl was unexplored?...

BÉRENGER: No. The place. The girl, if you like, too!

ÉDOUARD: You're always searching for something out of the
way. Always aiming at something out of reach.

BÉRENGER: But I tell you it wasn't. This girl...

ÉDOUARD: The answer is that it *is,* and so is *she* now. Your problems are so complicated, so impractical. You've always been
dissatisfied, always refused to resign yourself.

BÉRENGER: That's because I'm suffocating... The air I have to
breathe is not the kind that's made for me.

ÉDOUARD: [*clearing his throat*] Think yourself lucky you don't
suffer from ill-health, you're not a sick man or an invalid.

BÉRENGER: [*without paying attention to what* ÉDOUARD *is saying*]
No. No. I've seen it, I thought I'd got somewhere... some-

where like a different universe. Yes, only beauty can make the spring flowers bloom eternally... everlasting flowers... but I'm sorry to say it was only light that lied!... Once again everything fell into chaos... in a flash, in a flash! The same collapse, again and again... [*All this is said in a declamatory tone half way between sincerity and parody.*]

ÉDOUARD: You think only of yourself.

BÉRENGER: [*with slight irritation*] That's not true! Not true. I don't just think of myself. It's not for myself... not only for myself that I'm suffering right now, that I refuse to accept things! There comes a time when they're too horrible, and you can't...

ÉDOUARD: But that's the way of the world. Think of me, I'm a sick man... I've come to terms...

BÉRENGER: [*interrupting him*] It weighs on you, it weighs on you terribly, especially when you think you've seen... when you've thought you could hope... Oh!... then you can't go on... I'm tired... she's dead and they're dead and they'll all be killed... no one can stop it.

ÉDOUARD: But how did she die, this fiancée who perhaps wasn't? And who else is going to be killed, apart from the ones who usually get killed? What in fact are you talking about? Is it your dreams that are being killed? Generalities don't mean a thing.

BÉRENGER: I'm not talking through my hat...

ÉDOUARD: I'm sorry. I just can't understand you. I don't...

BÉRENGER: You're always wrapped up in your own little world. You never know anything. Where have you been living?

ÉDOUARD: Tell me about it then, give me some details.

BÉRENGER: It's absolutely incredible. There is in our town, though you're not aware of it, one beautiful district.

ÉDOUARD: Well?

BÉRENGER: Yes, there's one beautiful district. I've found it, I've just come from there. It's called the radiant city.

ÉDOUARD: Well, well!

BÉRENGER: In spite of it's name it's not a model neighbourhood, a happy or a perfect one. A criminal, an insatiable murderer, has turned it into hell.

ÉDOUARD: [coughing] I'm sorry, I can't help coughing!

BÉRENGER: You heard what I said?

ÉDOUARD: Perfectly: a murderer's turned it into hell.

BÉRENGER: He terrorizes and kills everyone. The district's getting deserted. It'll soon cease to exist.

ÉDOUARD: Oh yes, of course. I know! It must be that beggar who shows people the Colonel's photo and while they're looking at it throws them in the water! It's a trick to catch a fool. I thought you meant something else. If that's all it is...

BÉRENGER: [surprised] You knew? Knew all about it?

ÉDOUARD: Of course, I've known for a long time. I thought you were going to tell me something fresh, that there was another beautiful district.

BÉRENGER: Why did you never tell me anything about it?

ÉDOUARD: I didn't think there was any point. The whole town knows the story. I'm surprised even, you didn't know about it before, it's old news. Who doesn't know?... There didn't seem any need to tell you.

BÉRENGER: What? You mean everyone knows?

ÉDOUARD: That's what I said. You see, even I knew. It's a known fact, accepted and filed away. Even the schoolchildren know.

BÉRENGER: Even the schoolchildren?... Are you sure?

ÉDOUARD: Of course I am. [He clears his throat.]

BÉRENGER: How could children at school have found out?...

ÉDOUARD: Must have heard their parents talking... or grandparents... the schoolmaster too when he teaches them to read and write... Would you give me a little more rum?... Or perhaps not, it's so bad for me... I'd better go without. [Taking up his explanation again:] It's a pity, I agree.

BÉRENGER: A great pity! A terrible pity...

ÉDOUARD: What can we do about it?

BÉRENGER: Now it's my turn to say how very surprised I am to see you taking the matter so calmly... I always thought you were a sensitive, humane man.

ÉDOUARD: Perhaps I am.

BÉRENGER: But it's atrocious. Atrocious.

ÉDOUARD: I agree, I don't deny it.

BÉRENGER: Your indifference makes me sick! And I don't mind saying it to your face.

ÉDOUARD: Well you know... I...

BÉRENGER: [*louder*] Your indifference makes me sick!

ÉDOUARD: Don't forget... this is all new to you...

BÉRENGER: That's no excuse. You disappoint me, Édouard, frankly you disappoint me...

[ÉDOUARD *has a violent bout of coughing; he spits into his handkerchief.* BÉRENGER *rushes up to* ÉDOUARD, *who nearly collapses.*] You're really ill.

ÉDOUARD: A glass of water.

BÉRENGER: At once. I'll go and fetch one. [*Supporting him.*] Lie down here... on the couch...

ÉDOUARD: [*between coughs*] My briefcase... [BÉRENGER *bends down to pick up* ÉDOUARD'*s briefcase. In spite of his state of collapse,* ÉDOUARD *springs away from* BÉRENGER *to get hold of it himself.*] No... let me... [*He takes the briefcase from* BÉRENGER'*s hand, then, still weak and supported by* BÉRENGER, *he reaches the couch, still clinging to the briefcase, and lies down with* BÉRENGER'*s help, the briefcase at his side.*]

BÉRENGER: You're soaked in perspiration...

ÉDOUARD: And frozen stiff as well, oh... this cough... it's awful...

BÉRENGER: You mustn't catch cold. Would you like a blanket?

ÉDOUARD: [*shivering*] Don't worry. It's nothing... it'll pass...

BÉRENGER: Settle down and rest.

ÉDOUARD: A glass of water.

BÉRENGER: At once... I'll fetch one.

[*He hurries out to fetch a glass of water; you can hear the water running at the tap. Meanwhile* ÉDOUARD *raises himself on one*

*elbow and stops coughing; with one anxious hand he checks the
lock of his enormous black briefcase, and then, somewhat relieved,
lies back again still coughing but not so loudly.* ÉDOUARD *must
not give the impression he is trying to deceive* BÉRENGER: *he is
really ill and he has other worries, his briefcase for example. He
wipes his brow.* BÉRENGER *returns with the glass of water.*]
Feel better?

ÉDOUARD: Thanks... [*He takes a sip of the water and* BÉRENGER
takes the glass from him.] I'm sorry, it's stupid of me. I'm all
right now.

BÉRENGER: I'm the one to say I'm sorry. I should have realized...
When you're ill yourself, when you're really a sick man, like
you, it's hard to get carried away by something else... I've not
been fair to you. After all, these terrible crimes in the radiant
city might be the cause of your illness. It must have affected
you, consciously or otherwise. Yes, I'm sure it's that that's
eating you away. I confess it's wrong to pass judgment too
lightly. You can't know people's hearts...

ÉDOUARD: [*getting up*] I'm freezing here...

BÉRENGER: Don't get up. I'll go and fetch a blanket.

ÉDOUARD: I'd rather we went for a little walk, for the fresh air.
I waited for you too long in this cold. I'm sure it's warmer
outside.

BÉRENGER: I'm so tired emotionally, so depressed. I'd rather
have gone to bed... Still, if that's what you really want, I
don't mind coming with you for a while!

ÉDOUARD: That's very charitable of you!

[ÉDOUARD *puts his black-ribboned felt hat on again, buttons his
dark overcoat and dusts it down, while* BÉRENGER *also puts his hat
on.* ÉDOUARD *picks up his heavy, bulging black briefcase.*
BÉRENGER *walks in front of him, turning his back to* ÉDOUARD,
*who, as he passes the table, lifts the briefcase over it. As he does so,
the briefcase opens and a part of the contents spill over the table:
at first, large photographs.*]
My briefcase!

BÉRENGER: [*turning round at the noise*] What the... ah!

[*They both make a quick movement to the briefcase at the same time.*]

ÉDOUARD: Leave it to me.

BÉRENGER: No, wait, I'll help you... [*He sees the photos.*] But... but... what have you got there?

[*He picks up one of the photos. ÉDOUARD tries, but without appearing too alarmed, to take it back from him, to hide the other photos falling from his briefcase with his hands, and push them back. BÉRENGER, who has held on to the photo, looks at it in spite of ÉDOUARD's opposition.*]

What is it?

ÉDOUARD: I expect it's a photo... some photos...

BÉRENGER: [*still holding the photo and inspecting it*] It's an army man, with a moustache and pips... A Colonel with his decorations, the Military Cross... [*He picks up other photos.*] More photos! And always the same face.

ÉDOUARD: [*also looking*] Yes... it is... it's a Colonel. [*He seems to be trying to lay his hands on the photos; meanwhile a lot of others keep on pouring over the table.*]

BÉRENGER: [*with authority*] Let me see! [*He dives into the briefcase, pulls out more photos and looks at one:*] Quite a nice face. With the kind of expression that makes you feel sorry for him. [*He takes out more photos. ÉDOUARD mops his brow.*] What *is* all this? Why, it's the photo, the famous photo of the Colonel! You had it in there... you never told me!

ÉDOUARD: I'm not always looking inside my briefcase!

BÉRENGER: But it *is* your briefcase all right, you're never without it.

ÉDOUARD: That's no reason...

BÉRENGER: Oh well... We'll take the opportunity, while we're at it, of having another look!

[*BÉRENGER sticks his hands into the huge black briefcase. ÉDOUARD does the same with his own too-white hand, whose twisted fingers are now very clearly visible.*]

More photos of the Colonel... and more... and more...
[*To* ÉDOUARD, *who is now taking things out of the briefcase too,
and looking astonished:*] What are these?

ÉDOUARD: You can see, they're artificial flowers.

BÉRENGER: There are masses of them!... And these... Look,
dirty pictures... [*He inspects them while* ÉDOUARD *goes and
looks over his shoulder:*] Nasty!

ÉDOUARD: Excuse me! [*He takes a step away.*]

BÉRENGER: [*discarding the obscene photos and continuing his inventory*]
Some sweets... money-boxes... [*They both take from the
briefcase a heterogeneous collection of articles.*]... children's
watches!... What are they doing here?

ÉDOUARD: [*stammering*] I... I don't know... I tell you...

BÉRENGER: What do you make of it?

ÉDOUARD: Nothing. What *can* you make of it?

BÉRENGER: [*still taking from the briefcase, which is like a conjurer's
bottomless bag, an amazing quantity of all types of objects, which
cover the whole surface of the table and even fall on the floor*]...
pins... and more pins... pen-holders... and these... and
these... what's that?

   [*Much should be made of this scene: some of the objects can fly
   away on their own, others can be thrown by* BÉRENGER *to the four
   corners of the stage.*]

ÉDOUARD: That?... I don't know... I don't know at all... I
know nothing about it.

BÉRENGER: [*showing him a box*] What on earth's this?

ÉDOUARD: [*taking it in his hand*] Looks to me like a box, isn't it?

BÉRENGER: It is. A cardboard box. What's inside?

ÉDOUARD: I don't know. I don't know. I couldn't tell you.

BÉRENGER: Open it, go on, open it.

ÉDOUARD: [*almost indifferently*] If you like... [*He opens the box.*]
Nothing there! Oh yes, another box... [*He takes the small
box out.*]

BÉRENGER: And that box?

ÉDOUARD: See for yourself.

BÉRENGER: [*taking a third box from the second box*] Another box. [*He looks into the third box.*] Inside there's another box. [*He takes it out.*] And another inside that... [*He looks into the fourth box.*] And another box inside that... and so on, ad infinitum! Let's look again...

ÉDOUARD: Oh, if you want... But it'll stop us going for a walk...

BÉRENGER: [*taking boxes out*] Box... after box... after box... after box... after box...!

ÉDOUARD: Nothing but boxes...

BÉRENGER: [*taking a handful of cigarettes from the briefcase*] Cigarettes!

ÉDOUARD: Those belong to me! [*He starts collecting them, then stops.*] Take one if you like...

BÉRENGER: Thanks, I don't smoke.

[ÉDOUARD *puts a handful of cigarettes in his pocket, while others scatter over the table and fall on the floor.* BÉRENGER *stares at* ÉDOUARD:]

These things belong to that monster! You had them in here!

ÉDOUARD: I didn't know, I didn't know about it! [*He goes to take the briefcase back.*]

BÉRENGER: No, no. Empty it all! Go on!

ÉDOUARD: It makes me tired. You can do it yourself, but I don't see what use it is. [*He passes him the gaping briefcase.*]

BÉRENGER: [*taking another box out*] It's only another box.

ÉDOUARD: I told you.

BÉRENGER: [*looking inside the empty briefcase*] There's nothing else.

ÉDOUARD: Can I put the things back? [*He begins picking up the objects and putting them back in the briefcase, higgledy-piggledy.*]

BÉRENGER: The monster's things! Those are the monster's things. It's extraordinary...

ÉDOUARD: [*as before*] Er... yes... there's no denying it... It's true.

BÉRENGER: How do they come to be in your briefcase?

ÉDOUARD: Really... I... What do you expect me to say?...

You can't always explain everything... May I put them back?

BÉRENGER: I suppose so, yes, why not... What good could they be to us? [*He begins helping* ÉDOUARD *to fill the briefcase with the things he has taken out; then suddenly, as he is about to put back the last box, the one he did not examine, it opens and scatters over the table all kinds of documents as well as several dozen visiting cards. All this is in the style of a conjuring trick.*] Look, visiting cards.

ÉDOUARD: Yes. Visiting cards. So they are, how amazing... well I never!

BÉRENGER: [*inspecting the visiting cards*] That must be his name...

ÉDOUARD: Whose name?

BÉRENGER: The criminal's name, of course, the criminal's name!

ÉDOUARD: You think so?

BÉRENGER: It seems obvious to me.

ÉDOUARD: Really, why?

BÉRENGER: You can see for yourself, can't you! All the visiting cards have the same name. Look and read! [*He offers* ÉDOUARD *a few of the cards.*]

ÉDOUARD: [*reading the name written on the cards*] You're right... the same name... the same name on them all... It's quite true!

BÉRENGER: Ah... but... my dear Édouard, this is getting more and more peculiar, yes, [*Looking at him:*] more and more peculiar!

ÉDOUARD: You don't think...

BÉRENGER: [*taking the objects he mentions from the box*] And here's his address...

[ÉDOUARD *gently clears his throat, appearing slightly worried.*] And his identity card... a photo of him!... It's him all right... His own photo clipped to the Colonel's. [*With growing excitement:*] An address book... with the names and addresses... of all his victims!... We'll catch him, Édouard, we'll catch him!

ÉDOUARD: [*suddenly producing a neat little box; he could take it from his pocket or from one of his sleeves, like a conjuror, a folding box perhaps, which he flicks into shape as he shows it*] There's this too...

BÉRENGER: [*excited*] Quick, show me! [*He opens the little box and takes out more documents, which he lays out on the table.*] A note-book... [*He turns the pages:*] 'January 13th; today I shall kill... January 14th, yesterday evening I pushed an old woman with goldrimmed spectacles into the lake...' It's his private diary! [*He eagerly turns the pages, while* ÉDOUARD *appears very uneasy.*] 'January 23rd, nothing to kill today. January 25th, nothing to get my teeth into today either...'

ÉDOUARD: [*timidly*] Aren't we being indiscreet?

BÉRENGER: [*continuing*] 'January 26th, yesterday evening, just when I'd given up hope and was getting bored stiff, I managed to persuade two people to look at the Colonel's photo near the pool... February, tomorrow I think I'll be able to persuade a young blonde girl I've been after for some time to look at the photo...' Ah, that must be Dany, my poor fiancée...

ÉDOUARD: Seems quite likely.

BÉRENGER: [*still turning the pages*] Why look, Édouard, look, it's incredible...

ÉDOUARD: [*reading over* BÉRENGER'*s shoulder*] Criminology. Does that mean something?

BÉRENGER: It means it's an essay on crime... Now we've got his profession of faith, his credo... Here it is, you see. Have a look...

ÉDOUARD: [*as before: reading*] A detailed confession.

BÉRENGER: We've got him, the devil!

ÉDOUARD: [*as before: reading*] Future projects. Plan of campaign.

BÉRENGER: Dany, dear Dany, you'll be revenged. [*To* ÉDOUARD:] That's all the proof you need. We can have him arrested. Do you realize?

ÉDOUARD: [*stammering*] I didn't know... I didn't know...

BÉRENGER: So many human lives you could have saved.

ÉDOUARD: [*as before*] Yes... I see now. I feel awful about it. I didn't know. I never know what I've got in my briefcase, I never look inside.

BÉRENGER: Carelessness like that is unforgivable.

ÉDOUARD: It's true, forgive me, I'm so sorry.

BÉRENGER: After all, you don't mean to say these things got here all by themselves! You must have found them or been given them.

ÉDOUARD: [*coughing, mopping his brow and staggering*] I'm ashamed... I can't explain... I don't understand... I...

BÉRENGER: Don't blush. I'm really sorry for you, old chap. Don't you realize you're partly responsible for Dany's murder... and for so many others?

EDOUARD: I'm sorry... I didn't know.

BÉRENGER: Let's see what's to be done now. [*Heavy sigh.*] I'm afraid it's no good regretting the past. Feeling sorry won't help.

ÉDOUARD: You're right, you're right, you're right. [*Then, making an effort of memory:*] Ah yes, I remember now. It's funny, well, no, I suppose it isn't funny. The criminal sent me his private diary, his notes and index cards a very long time ago, asking me to publish them in a literary journal. That was before the murders were committed.

BÉRENGER: And yet he notes down what he's just done... In detail... It's like a log-book.

ÉDOUARD: No, no. Just then, they were only projects... imaginary projects. I'd forgotten the whole affair. I don't think he really intended to carry out all those crimes. His imagination carried him away. It's only later he must have thought of putting his plans into operation. *I* took them all for idle dreams of no importance...

BÉRENGER: [*raising his arms to Heaven*] You're so *innocent!*

ÉDOUARD: [*continuing*] Something like a murder story, poetry or literature...

BÉRENGER: Literature can lead anywhere. Didn't you know that?

ÉDOUARD: We can't stop writers writing, or poets dreaming.

BÉRENGER: We ought to.

ÉDOUARD: I'm sorry I didn't give it more thought and see the connection between these documents and what's been happening...

[*While talking,* ÉDOUARD *and* BÉRENGER *start making an attempt to collect and restore to the briefcase the various objects scattered over the table, the floor and the other pieces of furniture.*]

BÉRENGER: [*putting things back in the briefcase*] And yet the connection is simply between the intention and the act, no more no less, it's clear as daylight...

ÉDOUARD: [*taking a big envelope from his pocket*] There's still this!

BÉRENGER: What is it? [*They open the envelope:*] Ah, it's a map, a plan... Those crosses on it, what do they mean?

ÉDOUARD: I think... why yes... they're the places where the murderer's meant to be...

BÉRENGER: [*inspecting the map, which is spread right out on the table*] And this? Nine fifteen, thirteen twenty-seven, fifteen forty-five, nineteen three...

ÉDOUARD: Probably his timetable. Fixed in advance. Place by place, hour by hour, minute by minute.

BÉRENGER: ... Twenty-three hours, nine minutes, two seconds...

ÉDOUARD: Second by second. He doesn't waste time. [*He says this with a mixture of admiration and indifference.*]

BÉRENGER: Let's not waste ours either. It's easy. We notify the police. Then they just have to pick him up. But we must hurry, the offices of the Prefecture close before nightfall. Then there's no one there. Between now and tomorrow he might alter his plan. Let's go quickly and see the Architect, the Superintendent.

ÉDOUARD: You're becoming quite a man of action. *I*...

BÉRENGER: [*continuing*] We'll show him the proof!

ÉDOUARD: [*rather weakly*] I'll come if you like.

BÉRENGER: [*excited*] Let's go, then. Not a moment to lose! We'll finish putting all this away.

[*They pile the objects as best they can into the huge briefcase, into their pockets and the lining of their hats.*]

Mustn't forget any of the documents... quick.

ÉDOUARD: [*still more weakly*] Yes, all right.

BÉRENGER: [*who has finished filling the briefcase, although there could still be several visiting cards and other objects on the floor and the table*] Quick, don't go to sleep, quick, quick... We need all the evidence... Now then, close it properly... lock it...

[ÉDOUARD, *who is rather harassed, tries in vain to lock the briefcase with a small key; he is interrupted by a fit of coughing.*]

Double lock it!... This is no time for coughing!

[ÉDOUARD *goes on trying and struggles not to cough*].

BÉRENGER: Oh God, how clumsy you are, you've no strength in your fingers. Put some life into it, come on!... Get a move on. Oh, give it to me! [*He takes the briefcase and the key from* ÉDOUARD.]

ÉDOUARD: I'm sorry, I'm not very good with my hands...

BÉRENGER: It's *your* briefcase and you don't even know how to close it... Let me have the key, can't you.

[*He snatches the key quite roughly from* ÉDOUARD, *who had taken it back from him.*]

ÉDOUARD: Take it then, here you are, there.

BÉRENGER: [*fastening the briefcase*] How do you think you can close it without a key? That's it. Keep it...

ÉDOUARD: Thank you.

BÉRENGER: Put it in your pocket or you'll lose it.

[ÉDOUARD *obeys.*]

That's the way. Let's go... [*He makes for the door, reluctantly followed by* ÉDOUARD, *and turns round to say:*] Don't leave the light on, switch it off, please.

[ÉDOUARD *turns back and goes to switch off. To do this he sets the briefcase down near the chair: he will leave it behind.*]

Come on... Come on... Hurry up... Hurry... [*They both go out quickly. You can hear the door opening and slammed shut, then their footsteps in the entrance. While the noises of the town become audible again, you can see the two in the street. In their haste they bump into the* CONCIERGE, *who can be seen in front of the*

window. BÉRENGER *is pulling* ÉDOUARD *along by the hand.*]
CONCIERGE: [*who has just been knocked into, while* BÉRENGER *and* ÉDOUARD *disappear*] Of all the...! [*She goes on muttering, incomprehensibly.*]

CURTAIN

ACT THREE

A wide avenue in an outlying part of the town. At the back of the stage the view is masked by a raised pavement, a few yards wide, with a railing along the edge. Steps, also with a railing, leading up from street to pavement in full view of the audience. This short flight of stone steps should be like those in some of the old streets of Paris, such as the Rue Jean de Beauvais.

Later, at the back, there is a setting sun, large and red, but without brilliance: the light does not come from there.

So at the back of the stage it is as though there were a kind of wall, four and a half or six feet high, according to the height of the stage. In the second half of the act this wall will have to open to reveal a long street in perspective with some buildings in the distance: the buildings of the Prefecture.

To the right of the stage, in the foreground, a small bench.

Before the curtain rises you can hear shouts of 'Long live Mother Peep's geese! Long live Mother Peep's geese!'

The curtain goes up.

On the raised part of the stage, near the railing, is MOTHER PEEP, *a fat soul resembling the* CONCIERGE *of Act II. She is addressing a crowd which is out of sight: all you can see are two or three flags, with the device of a goose in the middle. The white goose stands out against the green background of the flags.*

PEEP: [*also carrying a green flag with a goose in the middle*] People, listen to me. I'm Mother Peep and I keep the public geese! I've a long experience of politics. Trust me with the chariot of state, drawn by my geese, so I can legislate. Vote for *me*. Give *me* your confidence. Me and my geese are asking for power. [*Shouts from the crowd, the flags are waved: 'Long live Mother Peep! Long live Mother Peep's geese!'* BÉRENGER *comes in from the right, followed by* ÉDOUARD, *who is out of breath.* BÉRENGER *drags him after him, pulling him by the sleeve. In this way they cross the stage from right to left and from left to right. During the dialogue between* ÉDOUARD *and* BÉRENGER, MOTHER PEEP *cannot be heard speaking, but she will be seen gesticulating and opening her mouth wide. The acclamation of the hidden crowd forms no more than a quiet background of sound.* MOTHER PEEP's *words and the sound of voices can of course be heard between the speeches of* ÉDOUARD *and* BÉRENGER.]

BÉRENGER: Come along, hurry up, do hurry up. Just one more effort. It's down there, right at the end. [*He points.*] Down there, the Prefecture buildings, we must arrive in time, before the offices close, in half an hour it'll be too late. The Architect, I mean the Superintendent, will have gone, and I've told you why we can't wait for tomorrow. Between now and then the killer might make off... or find some fresh victims! He must know I'm on his track.

ÉDOUARD: [*breathless but polite*] Wait a minute, please, you've made me run too fast.

PEEP: Fellow citizens, citizenesses...

BÉRENGER: Come on, come on.

ÉDOUARD: Let me have a rest... I can't keep going.

BÉRENGER: We haven't got time.

PEEP: Fellow citizens, citizenesses...

ÉDOUARD: I can't go on. [*He sits down on the bench.*]

BÉRENGER: All right, then. For one second, not more. [*He remains standing, near the bench.*] I wonder what all that crowd's for.

ÉDOUARD: Election meeting.

PEEP: Vote for us! Vote for us!

BÉRENGER: Looks like my concierge.

ÉDOUARD: You're seeing things. She's a politician, Mother Peep, a keeper of geese. A striking personality.

BÉRENGER: The name sounds familiar, but I've no time to listen.

ÉDOUARD: [*to* BÉRENGER] Sit down for a moment, you're tired.

PEEP: People, you are mystified. You shall be demystified.

BÉRENGER: [*to* ÉDOUARD] I haven't time to feel tired.

VOICE FROM THE CROWD: Down with mystification! Long live Mother Peep's geese!

ÉDOUARD: [*to* BÉRENGER] I'm sorry. Just a second. You said a second.

PEEP: I've raised a whole flock of demystifiers for you. They'll demystify you. But to demystify, you must first mystify. We need a new mystification.

BÉRENGER: We haven't time, we haven't time!

VOICE FROM THE CROWD: Up with the mystification of the demystifiers!

BÉRENGER: We haven't a moment to lose! [*He sits down all the same, consulting his watch:*] Time's getting on.

VOICE FROM THE CROWD: Up with the new mystification!

BÉRENGER: [*to* ÉDOUARD] Let's go.

ÉDOUARD: [*to* BÉRENGER] Don't worry. You know perfectly well the time's the same as it was just now.

PEEP: I promise you I'll change everything. And changing everything means changing nothing. You can change the names, but the things remain the same. The old mystifications haven't stood up to psychological and sociological analysis. The new one will be foolproof and cause nothing but misunderstanding. We'll bring the lie to perfection.

BÉRENGER: [*to* ÉDOUARD] Let's go!

ÉDOUARD: If you like.

BÉRENGER: [*noticing that* ÉDOUARD, *who is painfully rising to his feet, no longer has his briefcase*] Where's your briefcase?

ÉDOUARD: My briefcase? What briefcase? Ah yes, my briefcase. It must be on the bench. [*He looks on the bench.*] No. It's not on the bench.

BÉRENGER: It's extraordinary! You always have it with you!

ÉDOUARD: Perhaps it's *under* the bench.

PEEP: We're going to disalienate mankind.

BÉRENGER: [*to* ÉDOUARD] Look for it, why don't you look for it? [*They start looking for the briefcase under the bench, then on the floor of the stage.*]

PEEP: [*to crowd*] To disalienate mankind, we must alienate each individual man... and there'll be soup kitchens for all!

VOICE FROM THE CROWD: Soup kitchens for all and Mother Peep's geese!

BÉRENGER: [*to* ÉDOUARD] We must find it, hurry! Where could you have left it?

PEEP: [*to crowd, while* BÉRENGER *and* ÉDOUARD, *look for the briefcase, the former frantically, the latter apathetically*] We won't persecute, but we'll punish, and deal out justice. We won't colonize, we'll occupy the countries we liberate. We won't exploit men, we'll make them productive. We'll call compulsory work voluntary. War shall change its name to peace and everything will be altered, thanks to me and my geese.

BÉRENGER: [*still searching*] It's incredible, unbelievable, where can it have got to? I hope it hasn't been stolen. That would be a catastrophe, a catastrophe!

VOICE FROM THE CROWD: Long live Mother Peep's geese! Long live soup for the people!

PEEP: When tyranny is restored we'll call it discipline and liberty. The misfortune of one is the happiness of all.

BÉRENGER: [*to* ÉDOUARD] You don't realize, it's a disaster, we can't do a thing without proof, without the documents. They won't believe us.

ÉDOUARD: [*to* BÉRENGER, *nonchalantly*] Don't worry, we'll find it again. Let's look for it quietly. The great thing is to keep calm. [*They start searching again.*]

PEEP: [*to the crowd*] Our political methods will be more than scientific. They'll be para-scientific. Our reason will be founded on anger. And there'll be soup kitchens for all.

VOICE FROM THE CROWD: Long live Mother Peep! Long live the geese! Long live the geese!

VOICE FROM THE CROWD: And we'll be disalienated, thanks to Mother Peep.

PEEP: Objectivity is subjective in the para-scientific age.

BÉRENGER: [*wringing his hands, to* ÉDOUARD] It's one of the criminal's tricks.

ÉDOUARD: [*to* BÉRENGER] It's interesting, what Mother Peep says!

VOICE FROM THE CROWD: Long live Mother Peep!

BÉRENGER: [*to* ÉDOUARD] I tell you it's one of the criminal's tricks!

ÉDOUARD: [*to* BÉRENGER] You think so?
   [*From the left a man appears in top hat and tails, dead drunk, holding a briefcase.*]

MAN: I am... [*Hiccup*]... I am for... [*Hiccup*]... the re-habilitation of the hero.

BÉRENGER: [*noticing the man*] There it is! *He's* got it! [*He makes for the* MAN.]

ÉDOUARD: Long live Mother Peep!

BÉRENGER: Where did you find that briefcase? Give it back!

MAN: Don't you favour the rehabilitation of the hero?

PEEP: [*to the crowd*] As for the intellectuals...

BÉRENGER: [*trying to pull the briefcase away from the* MAN] Thief!... Let go of that briefcase!

PEEP: [*to the crowd*]We'll make them do the goose-step! Long live the geese!

MAN: [*between two hiccups, clinging on to the briefcase*] I didn't steal it. It's *my* briefcase.

VOICE FROM THE CROWD: Long live the geese!

BÉRENGER: [*to* MAN] Where did you get it from? Where did you buy it?

MAN: [*hiccuping while being shaken by* BÉRENGER, *to* ÉDOUARD] Are you sure it's your briefcase?

ÉDOUARD: I think so... Looks like it.

BÉRENGER: [*to* MAN] Give it back to me, then!

MAN: I'm for the hero!

BÉRENGER: [*to* ÉDOUARD] Help me! [BÉRENGER *tackles the* MAN.]

ÉDOUARD: Yes, of course. [*He goes up to the* MAN, *but lets* BÉ-RENGER *tackle him on his own. He is looking at* MOTHER PEEP.]

PEEP: While they're demystifying the mystifications demystified long ago, the intellectuals will give us a rest and leave *our* mystifications alone.

VOICE FROM THE CROWD: Long live Mother Peep!

MAN: I tell you it's mine!

PEEP: They'll be stupid, that means intelligent. Cowardly, that means brave. Clear-sighted, that means blind.

ÉDOUARD & VOICE FROM THE CROWD: Long live Mother Peep!

BÉRENGER: [*to* ÉDOUARD] This is no time to stand and gape. Leave Mother Peep alone.

ÉDOUARD: [*to* MAN, *coolly*] Give him the briefcase or else tell him where you bought it.

MAN: [*hiccup*] We need a hero!

BÉRENGER: [*to* MAN, *having at last managed to get hold of the briefcase*] What's inside?

MAN: I don't know. Papers.

BÉRENGER: [*opening the briefcase*] At last! Drunken sot.

ÉDOUARD: What do you mean by a hero?

PEEP: We'll march backwards and be in the forefront of history.

MAN: [*while* BÉRENGER *digs into the briefcase, and* ÉDOUARD *has a look over his shoulder, absentmindedly*] A hero? A man who dares to think against history and react against his times. [*Loudly*] Down with Mother Peep!

BÉRENGER: [*to* MAN] You're blind drunk!

MAN: A hero fights his own age and creates a different one.

BÉRENGER: [*taking bottles of wine out of the* MAN'*s briefcase*] Bottles of wine!

MAN: Half empty! That's not a crime!

PEEP: . . . for history has reason on its side. . .

MAN: [*pushed by* BÉRENGER, *he staggers and falls on his behind, exclaiming*] . . . when reason's lost its balance. . .

BÉRENGER: And are you reasonable to get drunk like this? [*To* ÉDOUARD:] Where the devil *is* your briefcase, then?

MAN: Didn't I tell you it was mine? Down with Mother Peep!

ÉDOUARD: [*still indifferent and without moving*] How do I know? You can see I'm looking for it.

VOICE FROM THE CROWD: Up Mother Peep! Up Mother Peep's geese! She changes everything by changing nothing.

BÉRENGER: [*to* ÉDOUARD] I shan't forgive you for this!

MAN: [*stumbling to his feet*] Down with Mother Peep!

ÉDOUARD: [*to* BÉRENGER, *snivelling*] Oh, don't go on at me! I'm not well.

BÉRENGER: [*to* ÉDOUARD] I can't help it, I'm sorry! Think of the state *I'm* in!

> [*At this moment a little* OLD MAN, *with a pointed white beard, who looks shy and is poorly dressed, comes in from the right, holding in one hand an umbrella and in the other a huge black briefcase, identical with the one* ÉDOUARD *had in Act II.*]

MAN: [*pointing to the* OLD MAN] There's your briefcase! That must be the one!

> [BÉRENGER *makes a dive at the* OLD MAN.]

PEEP: If an ideology doesn't apply to real life, we'll say it does and it'll all be perfect. The intellectuals will back us up. They'll find us anti-myths to set against the old ones. We'll replace the myths...

BÉRENGER: [*to* OLD MAN] I beg pardon, Monsieur.

PEEP: ... by slogans... and the latest platitudes!...

OLD MAN: [*raising his hat*] I beg pardon, Monsieur, can you tell me where the Danube is?

MAN: [*to* OLD MAN] Are you for the hero?

BÉRENGER: [*to* OLD MAN] Your briefcase looks just like my friend's. [*Pointing to him:*] Monsieur Édouard.

ÉDOUARD: [*to* OLD MAN] How do you do?

VOICE FROM THE CROWD: Up Mother Peep!

OLD MAN: [*to* ÉDOUARD] Danube Street, please?

BÉRENGER: Never mind about Danube Street.

OLD MAN: Not Danube *Street*. The Danube.

MAN: But this is Paris.

OLD MAN: [*to* MAN] I know. I *am* a Parisian.

BÉRENGER: [*to* OLD MAN] It's about the briefcase!

MAN: [*to* OLD MAN] He wants to see what you've got in your briefcase.

OLD MAN: That's nobody's business. I don't even ask myself. I'm not so inquisitive.

BÉRENGER: Of your own free will or by force you're going to show us...

[BÉRENGER, *the* MAN *and even* ÉDOUARD *try to take the brief-case from the* OLD MAN, *who fights back, protesting.*]

OLD MAN: [*struggling*] I won't let you!

PEEP: No more profiteers. It's me and my geese...

[*They are all round the* OLD MAN, *harrying him and trying to take the briefcase from him: the* MAN *manages to get it away from him first, then the* OLD MAN *snatches it back and* ÉDOUARD *lays hands on it, only to lose it again to the* OLD MAN: *they also get hold of the* MAN's *briefcase again, realize their mistake when they see the bottles and give it him back, etc.*]

BÉRENGER: [*to* ÉDOUARD] Idiot!

[*He gets hold of the briefcase, the* OLD MAN *takes it back again and the* MAN *takes it from him.*]

MAN: [*offering it to* ÉDOUARD] Here it is!

[*The* OLD MAN *snatches it and tries to run away, the others catch him, etc. Meanwhile* MOTHER PEEP *is continuing her speech:*]

PEEP ... me and my geese who'll dole out public property. Fair shares for all. I'll keep the lion's share for myself and my geese...

VOICE FROM THE CROWD: Up the geese!

PEEP: ... to give my geese more strength to draw the carts of state.

VOICE FROM THE CROWD: The lion's share for the geese! The lion's share for the geese!

MAN: [*shouting to* MOTHER PEEP] And we'll be free to criticize?

PEEP: Let's all do the goose-step!

VOICE FROM THE CROWD: The goose-step, the goose-step!

MAN: Free to criticize?

PEEP: [*turning to the* MAN] Everyone will be free to say if the goose-step's not well done!

> [*A kind of rhythmic marching is heard and the crowd shouting:* 'The goose-step, the goose-step!' *Meanwhile the* OLD MAN *has managed to escape with his briefcase. He goes off left followed by* BÉRENGER. ÉDOUARD, *who has made as if to follow* BÉRENGER *and the* OLD MAN, *turns back and goes to lie down on the bench, coughing. The* MAN *goes up to him.*]

MAN: [*to* ÉDOUARD] Aren't you well? Have a swig! [*He tries to offer him a half-empty bottle of wine.*]

ÉDOUARD: [*refusing*] No thank you.

MAN: Yes, yes. It'll do you good. Cheer you up.

ÉDOUARD: I don't want to be cheered up.

> [*The* MAN *makes the protesting* ÉDOUARD *drink; wine is spilt on the ground; the bottle too can fall and break. The* MAN *goes on making* ÉDOUARD *drink, while he speaks to* MOTHER PEEP:]

MAN: [*very drunk*] Science and art have done far more to change thinking than politics have. The real revolution is taking place in the scientists' laboratories and in the artists' studios. Einstein, Oppenheimer, Breton, Kandinsky, Picasso, Pavlov, they're the ones who are really responsible. They're extending our field of knowledge, renewing our vision of the world, transforming us. Soon the means of production will give everyone a chance to live. The problem of economics will settle itself. Revolutions are a barbarous weapon, myths and grudges that go off in your face. [*He takes another bottle of wine from his briefcase and has a good swig.*] Penicillin and the fight against dypsomania are worth more than politics and a change of government.

PEEP: [*to* MAN] Bastard! Drunkard! Enemy of the people! Enemy of history! [*To the crowd:*] I denounce this man: the drunkard, the enemy of history.

VOICE FROM THE CROWD: Down with history's enemy! Let's kill

the enemy of history!

ÉDOUARD: [*painfully getting up*] We are all going to die. That's the only alienation that counts!

BÉRENGER: [*comes in holding the* OLD MAN'*s briefcase*] There's nothing in the briefcase.

OLD MAN: [*following* BÉRENGER] Give it back to me, give it back!

MAN: I'm a hero! I'm a hero! [*He staggers quickly to the back of the stage and climbs up the stairs to* MOTHER PEEP.] I don't think like other people! I'm going to tell them!

BÉRENGER: [*to* OLD MAN] It's not Édouard's briefcase, here it is, I'm sorry.

ÉDOUARD: Don't go. It's heroism to think against your times, but madness to say so.

BÉRENGER: It's not *your* briefcase. So where the devil *is* yours? [*Meanwhile the* MAN *has reached the top of the steps, next to* MOTHER PEEP.]

PEEP: [*producing a huge briefcase, which has not been noticed up to now, and brandishing it*] Let's have a free discussion! [*She hits the* MAN *over the head with her briefcase.*] Rally round, my geese! Here's pasture for you!

[MOTHER PEEP *and the* MAN *fall struggling on the raised pavement. During the following scene either* MOTHER PEEP'*s head or the* MAN'*s or both at once will become visible, in the midst of a frightful hubbub of voices crying:* 'Up Mother Peep! Down with the drunk!' *Then, at the end of the following dialogue* MOTHER PEEP'*s head reappears alone, for the last time: it is hideous. Before disappearing, she says:* 'My geese have liquidated him. But only physically.' *Punch and Judy style.*]

ÉDOUARD: The wise man says nothing. [*To* OLD MAN:] Doesn't he, Monsieur?

BÉRENGER: [*wringing his hands*] But where is it? We must have it.

OLD MAN: Where are the banks of the Danube? You can tell me *now*.

[*He straightens his clothes, shuts his briefcase and takes back his umbrella.* MOTHER PEEP'*s briefcase has opened as she hit the* MAN *and rectangular cardboard boxes have fallen from it to the ground.*]

BÉRENGER: There's your briefcase, Édouard! It's Mother Peep's. [*He notices the boxes.*] And there are the documents.

ÉDOUARD: You think so?

OLD MAN: [*to* ÉDOUARD] Damn it, he's got a mania for running after briefcases! What's he looking for?

[BÉRENGER *bends down, picks up the boxes and then comes back to the front of the stage to* ÉDOUARD *and the* OLD MAN, *looking disappointed.*]

ÉDOUARD: It's my briefcase he wants to find!

BÉRENGER: [*showing the boxes*] It's not the documents! It's only the goose game!

OLD MAN: I haven't played that for a long time.

BÉRENGER: [*to* ÉDOUARD] It's no concern of yours! It's the briefcase we're after... the briefcase with the documents. [*To the* OLD MAN:] The evidence, to arrest the criminal!

OLD MAN: So that's it, you should have said so before.

[*It is at this moment that* MOTHER PEEP'*s head appears for the last time to make the remark already mentioned. Immediately afterwards the noise of the engine of a truck is heard, which drowns the voices of the crowd and the three characters on the stage, who go on talking and gesticulating without a word being heard. A* POLICE SERGEANT *appears, who should be unusually tall: with a white stick he taps the invisible people on the other side of the wall over the head.*]

POLICEMAN: [*only visible from head to waist, wielding the stick in one hand and blowing his whistle with the other*] Come along now, move on there. [*The crowd cries:* 'The Police, the Police. Up the Police.' *The* POLICEMAN *continues moving them on in the same way, so that the noise of the crowd gradually dies and fades right away. A huge military truck coming from the left blocks half the upper part of the stage.*]

ÉDOUARD: [*indifferently*] Look, an army truck!

BÉRENGER: [*to* ÉDOUARD] Never mind about that.

[*Another military truck coming from the opposite side blocks the other half of the upper part of the stage, just leaving enough room for the* POLICEMAN *in between the two trucks.*]

OLD MAN: [*to* BÉRENGER] You should have said you were looking for your friend's briefcase with the documents. I know where it is.

POLICEMAN: [*above, blowing his whistle, between the trucks*] Move along there, move along.

OLD MAN: [*to* BÉRENGER] Your friend must have left it at home, in your hurry to leave.

BÉRENGER: [*to* OLD MAN] How did you know?

ÉDOUARD: He's right, I should have thought! Were you watching us?

OLD MAN: Not at all. It's a simple deduction.

BÉRENGER: [*to* ÉDOUARD] Idiot!

ÉDOUARD: I'm sorry... We were in such a hurry!

[*A young* SOLDIER *gets out of the military truck, holding a bunch of red carnations. He uses it as a fan. He goes and sits on the top of the wall, the flowers in his hand, his legs dangling over the edge.*]

BÉRENGER: [*to* ÉDOUARD] Go and fetch it, go and fetch it at once! You're impossible! I'll go and warn the Superintendent, so he'll wait for us. Hurry and join me as soon as you can. The Prefecture's right at the end. In an affair like this I don't like being alone on the road. It's not pleasant. You understand?

ÉDOUARD: Of course I do, I understand. [*To* OLD MAN:] Thank you, Monsieur.

OLD MAN: [*to* BÉRENGER] Could you tell me now where the Danube Embankment is?

BÉRENGER: [*to* ÉDOUARD, *who hasn't moved*] Well, hurry up! Don't stand there! Come back quick.

ÉDOUARD: All right.

BÉRENGER: [*to* OLD MAN] I don't know, Monsieur, I'm sorry.

ÉDOUARD: [*making off very slowly to the right, where he disappears, saying nonchalantly*] All right, then, I'll hurry. I'll hurry. Won't be long. Won't be long.

BÉRENGER: [*to* OLD MAN] You must ask, ask a policeman!

[*On his way out* ÉDOUARD *nearly knocks into a* 2ND POLICE-
MAN, *who appears blowing his whistle and waving his white stick
about too : he should be immensely tall, perhaps he could walk on
stilts.*]

ÉDOUARD: [*dodging the* POLICEMAN, *who doesn't look at him*] Oh,
sorry! [*He disappears.*]

BÉRENGER: [*to* OLD MAN] There's one. You can find out.

OLD MAN: He's very busy. Do you think I dare?

BÉRENGER: Yes, of course, He's all right.

[BÉRENGER *goes to the back of the stage after crying one last time
after* ÉDOUARD: *'Hurry up!' The* OLD MAN *very shyly and
hesitantly approaches the* 2ND POLICEMAN.]

OLD MAN: [*timidly, to the* 2ND POLICEMAN] I beg your pardon! I beg your pardon!

BÉRENGER: [*he has gone right to the back of the stage and has one foot
on the first step of the stairs*] I must hurry!

1ST POL.: [*between two blasts, pointing his white stick down at*
BÉRENGER *to make him move away*] Move on, move on there.

BÉRENGER: It's terrible. What a traffic jam! I'll never, never get
there. [*Addressing first one, then the other* POLICEMAN:] It's a good
thing we've got you here to keep the traffic moving. You've
no idea what bad luck this hold-up is for me!

OLD MAN: [*to* 2ND POLICEMAN] Excuse me, please, Monsieur.
[*Before addressing the* POLICEMAN *the* OLD MAN *has respect-
fully removed his hat and made a low bow; the* POLICEMAN *takes
no notice, he is getting excited, making signals which are answered
by the* POLICEMAN *the other side of the wall with his white stick,
while he too energetically blows his whistle.* BÉRENGER *goes
frantically from one to the other.*]

BÉRENGER: [*to* 1ST POLICEMAN] Oh, hurry up, I've got to get
by. I've a very important mission. It's humanitarian.

1ST POL.: [*who goes on blowing and signing* BÉRENGER *on with his
stick*] Move along!

OLD MAN: [*to* 2ND POLICEMAN] Monsieur... [*To* BÉRENGER:]
He won't answer. He's too busy.

BÉRENGER: Oh, these trucks are here for good. [*He looks at his watch:*] Luckily, it's still the same time. [*To* OLD MAN:] Ask him, go on and ask him, he won't bite you.

OLD MAN: [*to* 2ND POLICEMAN, *still blowing his whistle*] -Please, Monsieur.

2ND POL.: [*to the* 1ST] Get them to go back! [*Sound of the engines of the still stationary trucks.*] Make them go forward! [*Same sound.*]

SOLDIER: [*to* BÉRENGER] If I knew the city I'd tell him the way. But I'm not a native.

BÉRENGER: [*to* OLD MAN] The policeman's bound to give you satisfaction. That's his privilege. Speak louder.

    [*The* SOLDIER *goes on fanning himself with his bunch of red flowers.*]

OLD MAN: [*to* 2ND POLICEMAN] I'm sorry, Monsieur, listen, Monsieur.

2ND POL. What?

OLD MAN: Monsieur, I'd like to ask you a simple question.

2ND POL.: [*sharply*] One minute! [*To* SOLDIER:] You, why have you left your truck, eh?

SOLDIER: I... I... but it's stopped!

BÉRENGER: [*aside*] Good Heavens, that Policeman's got the Superintendent's voice! Could it be him? [*He goes to have a closer look:*] No. He wasn't so tall.

2ND POL.: [*to* OLD MAN *again, while the other* POLICEMAN *is still controlling the traffic*] What's that you wanted, you there?

BÉRENGER: [*aside*] No, it's not him. His voice wasn't quite as hard as that.

OLD MAN: [*to* 2ND POLICEMAN] The Danube Embankment, please, Monsieur l'Agent, I'm sorry.

2ND POL.: [*his reply is aimed at the* OLD MAN *as well as the* 1ST POLICEMAN *and the invisible drivers of the two trucks; it precipitates a scene of general chaos, which should be comic, involving everyone; even the two trucks move*] To the left! To the right! Straight on! Straight back! Forward!

[*The* IST POLICEMAN, *the upper part of whom only is seen above, moves his head and white stick in obedience to his words:* BÉRENGER *makes parallel gestures, still standing on the same spot: the* SOLDIER *does the same with his bunch of flowers. The* OLD MAN *steps to the left, then to the right, then straight on, straight back and forward.*]

BÉRENGER: [*aside*] All the police have the same voice.

OLD MAN: [*returning to the* 2ND POLICEMAN] Excuse me, Monsieur, excuse me, I'm rather hard of hearing. I didn't quite understand which way you told me to go... for the Danube Embankment, please...

2ND POL.: [*to* OLD MAN] You trying to take a rise out of me? Oh no, there are *times*...

BÉRENGER: [*aside*] The Superintendent was much more pleasant...

2ND POL.: [*to* OLD MAN] Come on... Clear off... deaf or daft ... bugger off! [*Blasts on the whistle from the* 2ND POLICEMAN, *who starts dashing about and knocks into the* OLD MAN, *who drops his walking stick.*]

SOLDIER: [*on the steps*] Your stick, Monsieur.

OLD MAN: [*picking up his stick, to the* 2ND POLICEMAN] Don't lose your temper, Monsieur l'Agent, don't lose your temper! [*He is very frightened.*]

2ND POL.: [*still directing the traffic jam*] Left...

BÉRENGER: [*to* OLD MAN, *while the trucks move a little at the back of the stage, threatening for a moment to crush the* IST POLICEMAN] That policeman's behaviour is disgraceful!

IST POL.: Look out, half-wits!

BÉRENGER: [*to* OLD MAN]... after all, he has a duty to be polite to the public.

IST POL.: [*to the supposed drivers of the two trucks*] Left!

2ND POL.: [*as above*] Right!

BÉRENGER: [*to* OLD MAN] ... It must be part of their regulations! ... [*To the* SOLDIER:] Mustn't it?

IST POL.: [*as before*] Right!

SOLDIER: [*like a child*] I don't know... [*Fanning himself with his *flowers.*] *I've* got my flowers.

BÉRENGER: [*aside*] When I see his boss, the Architect, I'll tell him about it.

2ND POL.: [*as before*] Straight on!

OLD MAN: It doesn't matter, Monsieur l'Agent, I'm sorry... [*He goes out left.*]

2ND POL.: [*as before*] To the left, left!

BÉRENGER: [*while the* 2ND POLICEMAN *is saying faster and faster and more and more mechanically:* '*Straight on, left, right, straight on, forwards, backwards, etc....*' *and the* IST POLICEMAN *repeats his orders in the same way, turning his head from right to left etc. like a puppet*] I think, Soldier, we're too polite, far too nervous with the police. We've got them into bad habits, it's our fault!

SOLDIER: [*offering the bunch of flowers to* BÉRENGER, *who has come close to him and climbed up one or two steps*] See how good they smell!

BÉRENGER: No thank you, I don't.

SOLDIER: Can't you see they're carnations?

BÉRENGER: Yes, but that's not the point. I've simply got to keep going. This hold-up's a disaster!

2ND POL.: [*to* BÉRENGER, *then he goes towards the young* SOLDIER, *when* BÉRENGER *moves away from him*] Move on.

BÉRENGER: [*moving away from the* POLICEMAN *who has just addressed this order to him*] You don't like these trucks either, Monsieur l'Agent. I can see that in your face. And how right you are!

2ND POL.: [*to* IST POLICEMAN] Go on blowing your whistle for a minute.

[*The* IST POLICEMAN *goes on as before.*]

IST POL.: All right! Carry on!

BÉRENGER: [*to* 2ND POLICEMAN] The traffic's getting impossible. Especially when there are things... things that can't wait...

2ND POL.: [*to the* SOLDIER, *pointing at the bunch of red carnations the latter is still holding and fanning himself with*] Haven't you got anything better to do than play with that?

SOLDIER: [*politely*] I'm not doing any harm, Monsieur l'Agent, that's not stopping the trucks from moving.

2ND POL.: It puts a spoke in the wheels, wise guy! [*He slaps the* SOLDIER *across the face: the* SOLDIER *says nothing. The* POLICE-MAN *is so tall that he does not need to climb the steps to reach the* SOLDIER.]

BÉRENGER: [*aside, in the centre of the stage, indignantly*] Oh!

2ND POL.: [*snatching the flowers from the* SOLDIER *and hurling them into the wings*] Lunatic! Aren't you ashamed of yourself? Get back in that truck with your mates.

SOLDIER: All right, Monsieur l'Agent.

2ND POL.: [*to* SOLDIER] Look alive there, stupid bastard!

BÉRENGER: [*in the same position*] Going much too far!

SOLDIER: [*climbing back into the truck with the help of the* IST POLICEMAN's *fist and the* 2ND POLICEMAN's *stick*] Yes, all right, I will! [*He disappears into the truck.*]

BÉRENGER: [*in the same position*] Much too far!

2ND POL.: [*to the other invisible soldiers who are supposed to be in the trucks and who could perhaps be represented by puppets or simply be painted sitting on painted benches in the trucks*] You're blocking the road! We're fed up with your damned trucks!

BÉRENGER: [*aside, in same position*] In my view a country's done for if the police lays its hand... and its fingers on the Army.

2ND POL.: [*turning to* BÉRENGER] What's the matter with you? It's none of your business if...

BÉRENGER: But I didn't say anything, Monsieur l'Agent, not a thing...

2ND POL.: It's easy to guess what's going on in the minds of people of your type!

BÉRENGER: How do you know what I...

2ND POL.: Never you mind! You try and put your wrong thinking right.

BÉRENGER: [*stammering*] But it's not that, Monsieur, not that at all, you're mistaken, I'm sorry, I'd not... I'd never... on the contrary, I'd even...

2ND POL.: What are you up to here anyway? Where are your identification papers?

BÉRENGER: [*looking in his pockets*] Oh well, if that's what you want, Monsieur l'Agent... You've a right to see them...

2ND POL.: [*who is now in the centre of the stage, close to* BÉRENGER, *who naturally looks very small beside him*] Come on, quicker than that. I've no time to waste!

1ST POL.: [*still above, between the two trucks*] Hey! You leaving me on my own to unscramble this traffic? [*He blows his whistle.*]

2ND POL.: [*shouting to the* 1ST] Just a minute, I'm busy. [*To* BÉRENGER:] Quicker than that. Well, aren't they coming, those papers?

BÉRENGER: [*who has found his papers*] Here they are, Monsieur l'Agent.

2ND POL.: [*examining the papers, then returning them to* BÉRENGER] Well... All in order!

[*The* 1ST POLICEMAN *blows his whistle and waves his white stick. The truck engines are heard.*]

1ST POL.: [*to* 2ND] Doesn't matter. We'll get him yet, next time.

BÉRENGER: [*to* 2ND POLICEMAN, *taking his papers back*] Thanks very much, Monsieur l'Agent.

2ND POL.: You're welcome...

BÉRENGER: [*to* 2ND POLICEMAN, *who is about to move off*] Now you know who I am and all about my case, perhaps I can ask for your help and advice.

2ND POL.: I don't know about your case.

BÉRENGER: Yes, you do, Monsieur l'Agent. You must have realized I'm looking for the killer. What else could I be doing round here?

2ND POL.: Stopping me from controlling the traffic, for example.

BÉRENGER: [*without hearing the last remark*] We can lay hands on him, I've all the evidence... I mean, Édouard has, he's bringing it along in his briefcase... Theoretically I've got it... meanwhile I'm off to the Prefecture, and it's still a long way... Can you send someone with me?

2ND POL.: Hear that? He's got a nerve!

1ST POL.: [*interrupting his mime, to the* 2ND] Is he one of us? He an informer?

2ND POL.: [*to* 1ST] He's not even that! Who does he think he is! [*He blows his whistle for the traffic.*]

BÉRENGER: Listen to me, please, this is really serious. You've seen for yourself. I'm a respectable man.

2ND POL.: [*to* BÉRENGER] What's it all got to do with you, eh?

BÉRENGER: [*drawing himself up*] I beg your pardon, but I *am* a citizen, it matters to me, it concerns us all, we're all responsible for the crimes that... You see, I'm a really serious citizen.

2ND POL.: [*to* 1ST] Hear that? Likes to hear himself talk.

BÉRENGER: I'm asking you once more, Monsieur l'Agent! [*To the* 1ST:] I'm asking you, too!

1ST POL.: [*still busy with the traffic*] That's enough, now.

BÉRENGER: [*continuing, to* 2ND POLICEMAN] ... you, too: can you send someone with me to the Prefecture? I'm a friend of the Superintendent's, of the Architect's.

2ND POL.: That's not my department. I suppose even you can see I'm in 'traffic control'.

BÉRENGER: [*plucking up more courage*] I'm a friend of the Superintendent's...

2ND POL.: [*bending down to* BÉRENGER *and almost shouting in his ear*] I'm-in-traffic-control!

BÉRENGER: [*recoiling slightly*] Yes, I see, but... all the same... in the public interest... public safety, you know!

2ND POL.: Public safety? *We* look after that. When we've the time. Traffic comes first!

1ST POL.: What *is* this character? Reporter?

BÉRENGER: No, Messieurs, no, I'm *not* a reporter... Just a citizen, that's all...

1ST POL.: [*between two blasts on the whistle*] Has he got a camera?

BÉRENGER: No, Messieurs, I haven't, search me... [*He turns out his pockets.*] ... I'm *not* a reporter...

2ND POL.: [*to* BÉRENGER] Lucky you hadn't got it on you or I'd have smashed your face in!

BÉRENGER: I don't mind your threats. Public safety's more important than I am. He killed Dany too.

2ND POL.: Who's this Dany?

BÉRENGER: He killed her.

1ST POL.: [*between two blasts, signals and shouts of: Right! Left!*] It's his tart...

BÉRENGER: No, Monsieur, she's my fiancée. Or was to be.

2ND POL.: [*to* 1ST] That's it all right. He wants revenge on account of his tart!

BÉRENGER: The criminal must pay for his crime!

1ST POL.: Phew! They can talk themselves silly, some of them!

2ND POL.: [*louder, turning to* BÉRENGER *again*] It's not my racket, get it? I don't give a good goddam for your story. If you're one of the boss's pals, go and see him and leave me in goddam peace.

BÉRENGER: [*trying to argue*] Monsieur l'Agent... I... I...

2ND POL.: [*as before, while the* 1ST POLICEMAN *laughs sardonically*] I keep the peace, so leave *me* in peace! You know the way... [*He points to the back of the stage, blocked by the trucks.*] So bugger off, the road's clear!

BÉRENGER: Right, Monsieur l'Agent, right, Monsieur l'Agent!

2ND POL.: [*to* 1ST, *ironically*] Let the gentleman through!

[*As though by magic the trucks move back; the whole set at the back of the stage is movable, and so comes apart*]

Let the gentleman through!

[*The* 1ST POLICEMAN *has disappeared with the back wall and the trucks; now, at the back of the stage, you can see a very long street or avenue with the Prefecture buildings in the far distance against the setting sun. A miniature tram crosses the stage far away.*]

Let the gentleman through!

1ST POL.: [*whose face appears over the roof of one of the houses in the street that has just appeared*] Come on, get moving! [*He gestures to him to start moving and disappears.*]

BÉRENGER: That's just what I'm doing...

2ND POL.: [to BÉRENGER] I hate you!

[*It is the* 2ND POLICEMAN's *turn to make a sudden disappearance: the stage has got slightly darker.* BÉRENGER *is now alone.*]

BÉRENGER: [*calling after the* 2ND POLICEMAN, *who has just disappeared*] I've more right to say that than you have! Just now I haven't got time... But you haven't heard the last of me! [*He shouts after the vanished* POLICEMAN:] You-haven't-heard-the-last-of-me!!

[*The* ECHO *answers: last-of-me...*

BÉRENGER *is now quite alone on the stage. The miniature tram is no longer visible at the back. It is up to the producer, the designer and the electrician to bring out* BÉRENGER's *utter loneliness, the emptiness around him and the deserted avenue somewhere between town and country. A part of the mobile set could disappear completely to increase the area of the stage.* BÉRENGER *should appear to be walking for a long time in the ensuing scene; if there is no revolving stage he can make the steps without advancing. It might in fact be possible to have the walls back again to give the impression of a long, narrow passage, so that* BÉRENGER *seems to be walking into some ambush; the light does not change; it is twilight, with a red sun glowing at the back of the stage. Whether the stage is broad and open or reduced by flats to represent a long, narrow street, there is a still, timeless half-light.*

While he is walking, BÉRENGER *will grow more and more anxious; at the start, he sets off, or appears to, at a fast pace; then he takes to turning round more and more frequently until his walk has become hesitant; he looks to right and left, and then behind him again, so that in the end he appears to be on the point of flight, ready to turn back; but he controls himself with difficulty and after a great effort decides to go forward again; if the set is movable and can be changed without having to lower the curtain or the lights,* BÉRENGER *might just as well walk from one end of the stage to the other, and then come back, etc.*

Finally, he will advance cautiously, glancing all round him; and *yet, at the end of the Act when the last character in the play makes his appearance—or is first heard, or heard and seen at the same time—*BÉRENGER *will be taken by surprise: so this character should appear just when* BÉRENGER *is looking the other way. The appearance of this character must, however, be prepared for by* BÉRENGER *himself:* BÉRENGER'*s mounting anguish should make the audience aware that the character is getting nearer and nearer.*]

BÉRENGER: [*starting to walk, or appearing to, and at the same time turning his head in the direction of the* POLICEMEN *towards the wings on the right, and shaking his fist at them*] I can't do everything at once. Now for the murderer. It'll be your turn next. [*He walks in silence for a second or two, stepping it out.*] Outrageous attitude! I don't believe in reporting people, but I'll talk to the Chief Superintendent about it, you bet I will! [*He walks in silence.*] I hope I'm not too late! [*The noise of the wind: a dead leaf flutters down and* BÉRENGER *turns up his overcoat collar.*] And now, on top of everything else, the wind's got up. And the light's going. Will Édouard be able to catch me up in time? Will he catch me up in time? He's so slow! [*He walks on in silence while the set changes.*] Everything will have to be changed. First we must start by reforming the police force... All they're good for is teaching you manners, but when you really *need* them... when you want them to protect you... they couldn't care less... they let you down... [*He looks round:*] They and their trucks, they're a long way off already... Better hurry. [*He sets off again.*] I *must* get there before it's dark. It can't be too safe on the road. Still a long way... Not getting any nearer... I'm not making any progress. It's as though I wasn't moving at all. [*Silence*] There's no end to this avenue and its tramlines. [*Silence*] ... There's the boundary anyway, the start of the Outer Boulevards... [*He walks in silence.*] I'm shivering. Because of the cold wind. You'd think I was frightened, but I'm not. I'm used to being alone... [*He walks in silence.*] I've always been alone... And yet I love the human race, but at a distance. What's that matter, when I'm interested

in the fate of mankind? Fact is, I *am doing* something... [*He
smiles.*] Doing... acting... acting, not play-acting, doing!
Well, really I'm even running risks, you might say, for
mankind... and for Dany too. Risks? The Civil Service will
protect me. Dear Dany, those policemen defiled your memory.
I'll make them pay. [*He looks behind him, ahead, then behind
again; he stops.*] I'm half way there. Not quite. Nearly...
[*He sets off again at a not very determined pace; while he walks he
glances behind him:*] Édouard! That you, Édouard? [*The Echo
answers: ouard... ouard...*] No... it's not Édouard... Once
he's arrested, bound hand and foot, out of harm's way, the
spring will come back for ever, and every city will be radiant...
I shall have my reward. That's not what I'm after. To have
done my duty, that's enough... So long as it's not too late, so
long as it's not too late. [*Sound of the wind or the cry of an animal.*
BÉRENGER *stops.*] Supposing I went back... to look for
Édouard? We could go to the Prefecture tomorrow. Yes, I'll
go tomorrow, with Édouard... [*He turns in his tracks and takes
a step on the road back.*] No. Édouard's sure to catch me up in a
moment or two. [*To himself:*] Think of Dany. I must have
revenge for Dany. I must stop the rot. Yes, yes, I know I can.
Besides, I've gone too far now, it's darker that way than the
way I'm going. The road to the Prefecture is still the safest.
[*He shouts again:*] Édouard! Édouard!

ECHO: É-dou-ard... ou...ard...

BÉRENGER: Can't see now whether he's coming or not. Perhaps
he's quite near. Go on again. [*Setting off again with great
caution.*] Doesn't seem like it, but I've covered some ground...
Oh yes I have, no doubt about it... You wouldn't think so,
but I *am* advancing... advancing... Ploughed fields on my
right, and this deserted street... No risk of a traffic jam now
anyway, you can keep going. [*He laughs. The echo vaguely
repeats the laugh.* BÉRENGER, *scared, looks round:*] What's that?...
It's the echo... [*He resumes his walking.*] No one there, stupid
... Over there, who's that? There, behind that tree! [*He*

rushes behind a leafless tree, which could be part of the moving scene.] Why, no, it's nobody... [*The leaf of an old newspaper falls from the tree.*] Aah!... Afraid of a newspaper now. What a fool I am! [*He bursts out laughing. The echo repeats:... fool... I... am... and distorts the laugh.*] I must get further... I must go on! Advancing under cover of the Civil Service... advancing... I must... I must... [*Halt*] No, no. It's not worth it, in any case I'll arrive too late. Not my fault, it's the fault of the... fault of the... of the traffic, the hold-up made me late ... And above all it's Édouard's fault ... he forgets everything, every blessed thing... Perhaps the murderer will strike again tonight... [*With a start:*] I've simply got to stop him. I must go. I'm going. [*Another two or three paces in the direction of the supposed Prefecture:*] Come to think of it, it's all the same really, as it's too late. Another victim here or there, what's it matter in the state we're in... We'll go tomorrow, go tomorrow, Édouard and I, and much simpler that way, the offices will be closed this evening, perhaps they are already... What good would it do to... [*He shouts off right into the wings:*] Édouard! Édouard!

ECHO: É...ard...e...ard...

BÉRENGER: He won't come now. No point in thinking he will. It's too late. [*He looks at his watch:*] My watch has stopped... Never mind, there's no harm putting it off... I'll go tomorrow, with Édouard!... The Superintendent will arrest him tomorrow. [*He turns round.*] Where am I? I hope I can find my way home? It's in this direction! [*He turns round again quickly and suddenly sees the* KILLER *quite close to him.*] Ah!...

[*The set has of course stopped changing. In fact there is practically no scenery. All there is is a wall and a bench. The empty waste of a plain and a slight glow on the horizon. The two characters are picked out in a pale light, while the rest is in semi-darkness. Derisive laugh from the* KILLER: *he is very small and puny, illshaven, with a torn hat on his head and a shabby old gaberdine; he has only one eye, which shines with a steely glitter, and a set*

expression on his still face ; his toes are peeping out of the holes in
his old shoes. When the KILLER *appears, laughing derisively, he*
should be standing on the bench or perhaps somewhere on the wall :
he calmly jumps down and approaches BÉRENGER, *chuckling un-*
pleasantly, and it is at this moment that one notices how small he
is. Or possibly there is no Killer at all. BÉRENGER *could be*
talking to himself, alone in the half-light.]

It's him, it's the killer! [*To the* KILLER:] So it's you, then!

[*The* KILLER *chuckles softly :* BÉRENGER *glances round, anxi-*
ously.]

Nothing but the dark plain all around. . . You needn't tell me,
I can see that as well as you.

[*He looks towards the distant Prefecture. Soft chuckle from the*
KILLER.]

The Prefecture's too far away? That's what you just meant?
I know.

[*Chuckle from the* KILLER.]

Or was that me talking?

[*Chuckle from the* KILLER.]

You're laughing at me! I'll call the police and have you
arrested.

[*Chuckle from the* KILLER.]

It's no good, you mean, they wouldn't hear me?

[*The* KILLER *gets down from the bench or the wall and approaches*
BÉRENGER, *horribly detached and vaguely chuckling, both hands*
in his pockets. Aside :] Those dirty cops left me alone with
him on purpose. They wanted to make me believe it was
just a private feud.

[*To the* KILLER, *almost shouting :*] Why? Just tell me why?

[*The* KILLER *chuckles and gives a slight shrug of the shoulders :*
he is quite close to BÉRENGER, *who should appear not only bigger*
but also stronger than the almost dwarf-like KILLER. BÉRENGER
has a burst of nervous laughter.]

Oh, you really are rather puny, aren't you? Too puny to be a
criminal! I'm not afraid of you! Look at me, look how much

stronger I am. I could knock you down, knock you flying with a flick of my fingers. I could put you in my pocket. Do you realize?

[*Same chuckle from the* KILLER.]

I'm-not-afraid-of-you!

[*Chuckle from the* KILLER.]

I could squash you like a worm. But I won't. I want to understand. You're going to answer my questions. After all, you are a human being. You've got reasons, perhaps. You must explain, or else I don't know what... You're going to tell me why... Answer me!

[*The* KILLER *chuckles and gives a slight shrug of the shoulders.* BÉRENGER *should be pathetic and naive, rather ridiculous; his behaviour should seem sincere and grotesque at the same time, both pathetic and absurd. He speaks with an eloquence that should underline the tragically worthless and outdated commonplaces he is advancing.*]

Anyone who does what you do does it perhaps because... Listen... You've stopped me from being happy, and stopped a great many more... In that shining district of the town, which would surely have cast its radiance over the whole world... a new light radiating from France! If you've any feeling left for your country... it would have shone on you, would have moved you too, as well as countless others, would have made you happy in yourself... a question of waiting, it was only a matter of patience... *im*patience, that's what spoils everything... yes, you would have been happy, happiness would have come even to you, and it would have spread, perhaps you didn't know, perhaps you didn't believe it... You were wrong... Well, it's your own happiness you've destroyed as well as mine and that of all the others...

[*Slight chuckle from the* KILLER.]

I suppose you don't believe in happiness. You think happiness is impossible in this world? You want to destroy the world because you think it's doomed. Don't you? That's it, isn't it?

Answer me!

[*Chuckle from the* KILLER.]

I suppose you never thought for a single moment that you'd got it wrong. You were sure you were right. It's just your stupid pride. Before you finally make up your mind about this, at least let other people experiment for themselves. They're trying to realize a practical and technical ideal of happiness, here and now, on this earth of ours; and they'll succeed, perhaps, how can *you* tell? If they don't, then you can think again...

[*Chuckle from the* KILLER.]

You're a pessimist?

[*Chuckle from the* KILLER.]

You're a nihilist?

[*Chuckle from the* KILLER.]

An anarchist?

[*Chuckle from the* KILLER.]

Perhaps you don't like happiness? Perhaps happiness is different for you? Tell me your ideas about life. What's your philosophy? Your motives? Your aims? Answer me!

[*Chuckle from the* KILLER.]

Listen to me: you've hurt me personally in the worst possible way, destroying everything... all right, forget that... I'll not talk about myself. But you killed Dany! What had Dany done to you? She was a wonderful creature, with a few faults of course, I suppose she was rather hot-tempered, liked her own way, but she had a kind heart, and beauty like that is an excuse for anything! If you killed every girl who liked her own way just because she liked her own way, or the neighbours because they make a noise and keep you awake, or someone for holding different opinions from you, it would be ridiculous, wouldn't it? Yet that's what you do! Don't you? Don't you?

[*Chuckle from the* KILLER.]

We won't talk about Dany any more. She was my fiancée, and you might believe it's all just a personal matter. But tell me this... what had that Officer in the Engineers done to you, that Staff Officer?

[*Chuckle from the* KILLER.]

All right, I know... I understand, there are some people who hate a uniform. Rightly or wrongly they see it as the symbol of an abuse of power, of tyranny, and of war, which destroys civilizations. Right: we won't raise the question, it might take us too far, but that woman...

[*Chuckle from the* KILLER.]

...you know the one I mean, that young redhead, what had *she* done to you? What had you got against *her?* Answer me!

[*Chuckle from the* KILLER.]

We'll suppose you hate women, then: perhaps they betrayed you, didn't love you, because you're not, let's face it, you're not much to look at... it's not fair, I agree, but there's more than just the sexual side to life, there are some religious people who've given that up for all time... you can find satisfaction of a different kind in life and overcome that feeling of resentment...

[*Chuckle from the* KILLER.]

But the child, that child, what had he done to you? Children can't be guilty of anything, can they? You know the one I mean: the little fellow you pushed into the pool with the woman and the officer, poor little chap... our hopes are in the children, no one should touch a child; everyone agrees about that.

[*Chuckle from the* KILLER.]

Perhaps you think the human race is rotten in itself. Answer me!! You want to punish the human race even in a child, the least impure of all... We could debate the problem, if you like publicly, defend and oppose the motion, what do you say?

[*Chuckle from the* KILLER, *who shrugs his shoulders.*]

Perhaps you kill all these people out of kindness! To save them from suffering! For you, life is just suffering! Perhaps you want to cure people of the haunting fear of death? You think like

others before you, that man is and always will be the sick
animal, in spite of all social, technical or scientific progress, and
I suppose you want to carry out a sort of universal mercy-
killing? Well you're mistaken, you're wrong. Answer me!

[*Chuckle from the* KILLER.]

Anyway, if life's of little value, if it's too short, the suffering of
mankind will be short too: whether men suffer thirty or forty
years, ten years more or less, what's it matter to you? Let people
suffer if that's what they want. Let them suffer as long as they're
willing to suffer... Besides, time goes by, a few years hardly
count, they'll have a whole eternity of *not* suffering. Let them
die in their own time and it will all be over quite soon. Everything will flicker out and finish on its own. Don't hurry things
up, there's no point.

[*Chuckle from the* KILLER.]

Why, you're putting yourself in an absurd position, if you
think you're doing mankind a service by destroying it, you're
wrong, that's stupid! Aren't you afraid of ridicule? Eh?
Answer me that!

[*Chuckle from the* KILLER: *loud, nervous laugh from* BÉRENGER.
Then, after watching the KILLER *for a while :*]

I see this doesn't interest you. I haven't laid my finger on the
real problem, on the spot that really hurts. Tell me: do you
hate mankind? Do you hate mankind?

[*Chuckle from the* KILLER.]

But why? Answer me!

[*Chuckle from the* KILLER.]

If that *is* the case, don't vent your spleen on men, that's no
good, it only makes you suffer yourself, it hurts to hate, better
despise them, yes, I'll allow you to despise them, isolate yourself from them, go and live in the mountains, become a
shepherd, why not, and you'll live among sheep and dogs.

[*Chuckle from the* KILLER.]

You don't like animals either? You don't love anything that's
alive? Not even the plants?... What about stones and stars,

the sun and the blue sky?

[*Chuckle and shrug of the shoulders from the* KILLER.]

No. No, I'm being silly. One can't hate everything. Do you
believe society's rotten, that it can't be improved, that revo-
lutionaries are fools? Or do you believe the existence of the
universe is a mistake?

[*The* KILLER *shrugs his shoulders.*]

Why can't you answer me, answer me! Oh! Argument's impossible with you! Listen, you'll make me angry, I warn you!
No... no... I mustn't lose my self-control. I *must* understand
you. Don't look at me like that with your glittering eye. I'm
going to talk frankly. Just now I meant to have my revenge,
for myself and the others. I wanted to have you arrested, sent
to the guillotine. Vengeance is stupid. Punishment's not the
answer. I was furious with you. I was after your blood... as
soon as I saw you... not *immediately*, not that very moment,
no, but a few seconds later, I... it sounds silly, you won't
believe me, and yet I must tell you... yes... you're a human
being, we're the same species, we've got to understand each
other, it's our duty, a few seconds later, I loved you, or almost... because we're brothers, and if I hate *you*, I can't help
hating *myself*...

[*Chuckle from the* KILLER.]

Don't laugh: it exists, fellow feeling, the brotherhood of man,
I know it does, don't sneer...

[*Chuckle and shrug of the shoulders from the* KILLER.]

... ah... but you're a... you're nothing but a... now listen
to this. *We're* the strongest, *I'm* stronger physically than you
are, you're a helpless feeble little runt! What's more, I've the
law on my side... the police!

[*Chuckle from the* KILLER.]

Justice, the whole force of law and order!

[*Chuckle from the* KILLER.]

I mustn't, I *mustn't* get carried away... I'm sorry...

[*Chuckle from the* KILLER: BÉRENGER *mops his brow.*]

You've got more self-control than I have... but I'll calm down, I'll calm down... no need to be afraid... You don't *seem* very frightened... I mean, don't hold it against me... but you're not even scared, are you?... No, it's not that, that's not what I mean... Ah yes, yes... perhaps you don't realize. [*Very loud:*] Christ died on the Cross for *you*, it was for *you* he suffered, he *loves* you ... And you really need to be loved, though you think you don't!

[*Chuckle from the* KILLER.]

I swear to you that the blessed saints are pouring out tears for you, torrents and oceans of tears. You're soaked in their tears from head to foot, it's impossible for you not to feel a little wet!

[*Chuckle from the* KILLER.]

Stop sneering like that. You don't believe me, you don't believe me!... If Christ's not enough for you, I give you my solemn word I'll have an army of saviours climbing new Calvaries just for you, and have them crucified for love of you!... They must exist and I'll find them! Will that do?

[*Chuckle from the* KILLER.]

Do you want the whole world to destroy itself to give you a moment of happiness, to make you smile just once? That's possible too! I'm ready myself to embrace you, to be one of your comforters; I'll dress your wounds, because you *are* wounded, aren't you? You've suffered, haven't you? You're still suffering? I'll take pity on you, you know that now. Would you like me to wash your feet? Then perhaps you'd like some new shoes? You loathe sloppy sentimentality. Yes, I can see it's no good trying to touch your feelings. You don't want to be trapped by tenderness! You're afraid it'll make a fool of you. You've a temperament that's diametrically opposed to mine. All men are brothers, of course, they're like each other, but they're not always alike. And they've one thing in common. There must be one thing in common, a common language... What is it? What is it?

[*Chuckle from the* KILLER.]

Ah, I know now, I know... You see, I'm right not to give up hope for you. We can speak the language of reason. It's the language that suits you best. You're a scientific man, aren't you, a man of the modern era, I've guessed it now, haven't I, a cerebral man? You deny love, you doubt charity, it doesn't enter into your calculations, and you think charity's a cheat, don't you, don't you?

[*Chuckle from the* KILLER.]

I'm not blaming you. I don't despise you for that. After all, it's a point of view, a possible point of view, but between ourselves, listen here: what do you get out of all this? What good does it do *you*? Kill people if you like, but in your mind... leave them alive in the flesh.

[*Shrug of the shoulders and chuckle from the* KILLER.]

Oh, yes, in your opinion that would be a comic contradiction. Idealism you'd call it, you're for a practical philosophy, you're a man of action. Why not? But where's the action leading you? What's the final object? Have you asked yourself the question of ultimate ends?

[*A more accentuated chuckle and shrug of the shoulders from the* KILLER.]

It's an action that's utterly sterile in fact, it wears you out. It only brings trouble... Even if the police shut their eyes to it, which is what usually happens, what's the good of all the effort, the fatigue, the complicated preparations and exhausting nights on the watch... people's contempt for you? Perhaps you don't mind. You earn their fear, it's true, that's something. All right, but what do you do with it? It's not a form of capital. You don't even exploit it. Answer me!

[*Chuckle from the* KILLER.]

You're poor now, aren't you? Do you want some money? I can find you work, a decent job... No. You're not poor? Rich then?... Aaah, I see, neither rich nor poor!

[*Chuckle from the* KILLER.]

I see, you don't want to work: well, you shan't then. I'll look after you, or as I'm poor myself, I'd better say I'll arrange for me and my friends to club together, I'll talk to the Architect about it. And you'll lead a quiet life. We'll go to the cafés and the bars, and I'll introduce you to girls who aren't too difficult... Crime doesn't pay. So stop being a criminal and we'll pay you. It's only common sense.

[*Chuckle from the* KILLER.]

You agree? Answer, answer, can't you? You understand the language!... Listen I'm going to make you a painful confession. Often, I have my doubts about everything too. But don't tell anyone. I doubt the point of living, the meaning of life, doubt my own values and every kind of rational argument. I no longer know what to hang on to, perhaps there's no more truth or charity. But if that's the case, be philosophical; if all is vanity, if charity is vanity, crime's just vanity too... When you know everything's dust and ashes, you'd be a fool if you set any store by crime, for that would be setting store by life... That would mean you were taking things seriously... and then you'd be in complete contradiction with yourself. [*Gives nervous laugh:*] Eh? It's obvious. It's only logic, I caught you there. And then you'd be in a bad way, you'd be feeble-minded, a poor specimen. Logically we'd have the right to make fun of you! Do you want us to make fun of you? Of course you don't. You must have your pride, respect your own intelligence. There's nothing worse than being stupid. It's much more compromising than being a criminal, even madness has a halo round it. But to be stupid? To be ignorant? Who can accept that?

[*Chuckle from the* KILLER.]

Everyone will point at you and laugh!

[*Chuckle from the* KILLER: BÉRENGER *is obviously more and more baffled.*]

There's the idiot going by, there's the idiot! Ha! Ha! Ha!

[*Chuckle from the* KILLER.]

He kills people, gives himself all that trouble—Ha! Ha! Ha!—

and doesn't get anything out of it, it's all for nothing... Ha!
Ha! Do you want to hear that said, be taken for an idiot, an
idealist, a crank who 'believes' in something, who 'believes' in
crime, the simpleton! Ha! Ha! Ha!

[*Chuckle from the* KILLER.]

... Who believes in crime for its own sake! Ha! Ha! [*His
laugh suddenly freezes.*] Answer me! That's what they'll say,
yes... if there's anyone left to say it... [*Wrings his hands,
clasps them, kneels down and begs the* KILLER:] I don't know what
else I can say to you. We must have done something to hurt
you.

[*Chuckle from the* KILLER.]

Perhaps there's no wrong on our side.

[*Chuckle from the* KILLER.]

I don't know. It may be my fault, it may be yours. It may not
be yours or mine. It may not be anyone's fault. What you're
doing may be wrong or it may be right, or it may be neither
right nor wrong. I don't know how to tell. It's possible that
the survival of the human species is of no importance, so what
does it matter if it disappears... perhaps the whole universe is
no good and you're right to want to blast it all, or at least
nibble at it, creature by creature, piece by piece... or perhaps
that's wrong. I don't know any more, I just don't know. You
may be mistaken, perhaps mistakes don't really exist, perhaps
it's we who are mistaken to want to exist... say what you
believe, can't you? *I* can't, *I* can't.

[*Chuckle from the* KILLER.]

Some think just *being* is a mistake, an aberration.

[*Chuckle from the* KILLER.]

Perhaps your pretended motives are only a mask for the real
cause you unconsciously hide from yourself. Who knows.
Let's sweep all these reasons away and forget the trouble you've
already caused...

[*Chuckle from the* KILLER.]

Agreed? You kill without reason in that case, and I beg you, without reason I implore you, yes, please *stop*... There's no reason why you should, naturally, but please stop, just because there's *no reason* to kill or not to kill. You're killing people for nothing, save them for nothing. Leave people alone to live their stupid lives, leave them all alone, even the policemen... Promise me you'll stop for at least a month... *please* do as I ask, for a week, for forty-eight hours, to give us a chance to breathe... You will do that, won't you?...

[*The* KILLER *chuckles softly; very slowly he takes from his pocket a knife with a large shining blade and plays with it.*]

You filthy dirty moronic imbecile! You're ugly as a monkey! Fierce as a tiger, stupid as a mule...

[*Slight chuckle from the* KILLER.]

I'm on my knees, yes... but it's not to beg for mercy...

[*Slight chuckle from the* KILLER.]

It's to take better aim... I'm going to finish you, and then I'll stamp on you and squash you to pulp, you stinking rotten carcass of a hyena! [*Takes two pistols from his pockets and aims them at the* KILLER, *who doesn't move a muscle.*] I'll kill you, you're going to pay for it, I'll shoot and shoot, and then I'll hang you, I'll chop you into a thousand pieces, I'll throw your ashes into Hell with the excrement you came from, you vomit of Satan's mangy cur, criminal cretin...

[*The* KILLER *goes on playing with the blade of his knife; slight chuckle and shrug of the shoulders, but he does not move.*]

Don't look at me like that, I'm not afraid of you, you shame creation.

[BÉRENGER *aims without firing at the* KILLER, *who is two paces away, standing still, chuckling unpleasantly and quietly raising his knife.*]

Oh... how weak my strength is against your cold determination, your ruthlessness! And what good are bullets even, against the resistance of an infinitely stubborn will! [*With a start:*] But I'll get you, I'll get you...

[*Then, still in front of the* KILLER, *whose knife is raised and who is chuckling and quite motionless,* BÉRENGER *slowly lowers his two old-fashioned pistols, lays them on the ground, bends his head and then, on his knees with his head down and his arms hanging at his side, he stammers:*]

Oh God! There's nothing we can do. What can we do... What can we do...

[*While the* KILLER *draws nearer, still chuckling, but very very softly.*]

CURTAIN

London, August 1957

IMPROVISATION

or

THE SHEPHERD'S CHAMELEON

First produced in Paris by Maurice Jacquemont at the Studio des Champs Elysées, the 20th February, 1956. Set and costumes by Paul Coupille. Music adapted from 17th Century scores.

CHARACTERS:

> BARTHOLOMEUS I
> BARTHOLOMEUS II
> BARTHOLOMEUS III
> MARIE
> IONESCO

IONESCO *is asleep, his head on the table, surrounded with books and manuscripts. A ball-point pencil is sticking out of one hand. A bell rings.* IONESCO *snores. It rings again and then there is the sound of beating on the door and cries of: 'Ionesco! Ionesco!' Finally* IONESCO *jumps and rubs his eyes.*

MAN'S VOICE: Ionesco! Are you there?

IONESCO: Yes... Just a second!... What's the matter now? [*Smoothing his untidy hair* IONESCO *goes to the door and opens it.* BARTHOLOMEUS I *appears, in a scholar's gown.*]*

BART I: Morning, Ionesco.

IONESCO: Morning, Bartholomeus.

BART I: Glad I've found you in! I damned nearly went away and I'd have been very angry, specially as you haven't a phone... What on earth were you doing?

IONESCO: I was working, working... I was writing!

BART I: The new play? Is it ready? I'm waiting for it.

IONESCO: [*sitting in his armchair and motioning* BARTHOLOMEUS *to a*

---

* In the French production the gowns worn by the three Bartholomeus were the scholars' gowns of Molière's time. Tr.

chair] Sit down. [BARTHOLOMEUS *sits*.] Well, I'm working on it, you know. I've got right down to it. I feel quite overworked. It's coming along, but it's not easy. It's got to be perfect, hasn't it? No repetition, no dull passages... So you see I'm tightening, tightening it up...

BART I: You *have* finished it, then?... The first draft, let's see that...

IONESCO: But I tell you I'm still tightening the dialogue...

BART I: Do I understand you're tightening the dialogue before you've finished the play? I suppose that's *one* way of writing.

IONESCO: It's *my* way.

BART I: Now listen, have you finished the play or haven't you?

IONESCO: [*hunting amongst his papers on the table*] Yes... well no, you see... not exactly. It's here, of course, but I can't read it to you in its present state... so long as it's not...

BART I: ...finished... polished off!...

IONESCO: No, no... not polished off... polished, perfect! It's not the same thing at all.

BART I: Pity. We're going to miss a good chance. I've had a very interesting offer. A theatre that's dead keen on having one of your plays. The directors want it at once. They've asked me to take the job on and produce it according to the latest dramatic theories. Theories worthy of a people's theatre in this ultra-scientific age we live in. They'll bear all the costs, publicity and so on, providing the cast's limited to four or five and it won't cost too much to mount...

IONESCO: Tell them to be patient for a day or two. I promise I'll have tightened it all up by then... though, it's true, the season *is* getting on...

BART I: So long as the *play* is, we can still fix it up...

IONESCO: Which theatre is it?

BART I: A new theatre, with a scientific director and a young company of scientific actors who want to launch out with *you*. You'll get scientific treatment. The auditorium's not too big, seats for twenty-five and standing room for four... It's for a people's audience, but a select one.

IONESCO: Not too bad. If only we could fill it every evening!

BART I: Half fill it, even, and I'd be satisfied... Anyway, they want to start at once.

IONESCO: That'd be fine, if only the play was absolutely ready...

BART I: But you say it's practically all written!

IONESCO: Yes... yes... it is *practically* all written!

BART I: What's it all about? What's it called?

IONESCO: [*embarrassed and rather conceited*] Er... what's it about?... You want to know what it's about?... And what it's called?... Er... you know I never know how to talk about my plays... It's all in the dialogue, in the acting, in the stage effects, it's very visual, as usual... With me there's always first some image, some line or other which sets off the creative mechanism. And then I just let my own characters carry me along, I never know exactly where I'm going... For me every play is an adventure, a quest, the discovery of a universe that's suddenly revealed, and there's no one more surprised than I am to find that it exists...

BART I: We know all about that! Empirical stuff. You've explained it all before, dozens of times, in your previews, your articles and your interviews, about your creative mechanism, as you call it, though I don't like the word: 'creative'. 'Mechanism' is all right though. I like that.

IONESCO: [*naively*] That's true, I *have* talked about my, sorry, creative mechanism before. You've a good memory!

BART I: Tell me more about your new play. What was it this time, the initial image that set off the process of construction...

IONESCO: Well... er. Well... er... It's rather complicated, you know... That's a really sticky question!... Oh well, here goes! The title of my new play is: The Shepherd's Chameleon.

BART I: Why The Shepherd's Chameleon?

IONESCO: It's the crucial scene of the play, the motive force. Once, in a large country town, in the middle of the street, during the summer, I saw a young shepherd, about three o'clock in the afternoon, who was embracing a chameleon... It was such a touching scene I decided to turn it into a tragic farce.

BART I: That's feasible scientifically.

IONESCO: It'll only be the starting-point. I don't know yet whether you'll really see the shepherd embracing the chameleon on the stage, or whether I'll simply call the scene to mind... Whether it'll just be an invisible background... drama once removed... In fact, I think it will only have to serve as a pretext...

BART I: Pity. The scene somehow seemed to me to illustrate the reconciliation of the Self with the Other.

IONESCO: You see, this time I'm going to put myself in the play!

BART I: That's all you ever do.

IONESCO: It won't be the last time, then.

BART I: Well, which are you to be, the shepherd or the chameleon?

IONESCO: Oh no, definitely not the chameleon. *I* don't change colour every day... I'm not always being towed along by the latest fashion, like... but I'd rather not say who...

BART I: So you must be the shepherd then?

IONESCO: Not the shepherd either! I told you this was only a pretext, a starting point... In fact I put myself in the play to start off a discussion on the theatre, to reveal my own ideas...

BART I: As you're not a scholar, you've no right to have ideas... That's where I come in.

IONESCO: Let's say my experiences, then...

BART I: Scientific experiment's the only experience that's valid.

IONESCO: ... Well then... my beliefs...

BART I: Possible. But they're only provisional, we'll rectify them for you. Go on with your precarious exposition...

IONESCO: [*after a second's pause*] Thank you. You can say I *am* the shepherd if you like, and the theatre's the chameleon. Because *I've* embraced a theatrical career, and the theatre, of course, *changes*, for the theatre is life. It's changeable like life... The chameleon's life too!

BART I: I note the formula, which is almost a thought.

IONESCO: So I'll talk about the theatre, about dramatic criticism and the public...

BART I: You need to be more of a sociologist for that!

IONESCO: ... and the new drama, the essential character of which lies in its newness... I'll present my own points of view.

BART I: [*sweeping gesture*] Points of view with no optical instrument!

IONESCO: ... It'll be an improvisation.

BART I: Read me what you've written so far, anyway.

IONESCO: [*pretending to hold back*] It's not quite ready. I told you... the dialogue's not tightened up... Still, I could read you a short extract...

BART I: I'm listening to you. I'm here to pass judgment on you. And put you right.

IONESCO: [*scratching his head*] I always find it rather embarrassing, you know, to read out what I've written. My own text makes me sick...

BART I: Autocriticism does honour to the writer, dishonour to the critic.

IONESCO: All right, I'll read it to you anyhow, so you won't have come for nothing. [BART I *settles himself down comfortably*.] This is how the play starts. Scene One. Ionesco is asleep, his head on the table, surrounded with books and manuscripts. A ball-point pencil is sticking out of one hand. A bell rings. Ionesco snores. Then there is the sound of beating on the door and cries of: 'Ionesco! Ionesco!' Finally Ionesco jumps and rubs his eyes. Voice from outside the door: Ionesco! Are you there?' Ionesco: 'Yes... Just a second!.... What's the matter now?...' Smoothing his untidy hair [*With these words* IONESCO *makes the gesture.*] Ionesco goes to the door and opens it; Bartholomeus appears. Bartholomeus: 'Glad I've found you in! I damned nearly went away, and I'd have been very angry, specially as you haven't a phone. What on earth were you doing?' Ionesco: 'I was working, working, I was writing!...' Bartholomeus: 'The new play? Is it ready? I'm waiting for it!...' Ionesco, sitting in his armchair and motioning Bartholomeus to a chair: 'Sit down!'

[*While reading his play* IONESCO *sits down in his armchair as before. At this moment the bell is really heard to ring, followed by a beating on the door.*]

ANOTHER MAN'S VOICE: Ionesco! Are you there?

[BART I, *who has been nodding his head in approbation during the reading, glances over to the door where the Voice comes from.*]

IONESCO: Yes, just a second. What's the matter now?

[*Smoothing his untidy hair,* IONESCO *goes to the door and opens it.* BARTHOLOMEUS II *appears.*]

BART II: Morning, Ionesco.

IONESCO: Morning, Bartholomeus.

BART II: [*to* BART I] Well, Bartholomeus, how are you?

BART I: [*to* BART II] Well, Bartholomeus, how are you?

BART II: Glad I've found you in! I damned nearly went away, and I'd have been very angry, specially as you haven't a phone... What on earth were you doing?

IONESCO: I was working, working, I was writing... Sit down!

[*He indicates a chair to* BART II *and sits down himself. There is more knocking on the door and a third man's voice :*]

THIRD MAN'S VOICE: Ionesco! Ionesco! Are you there?

IONESCO: Yes, just a second! What's the matter now?

[IONESCO *stands up, smooths his hair, makes for the door and opens it.* BARTHOLOMEUS III *appears, in a scholar's gown, like the other two.*]

BART III: Morning, Ionesco.

IONESCO: Morning, Bartholomeus.

BART III: [*to* BART II] Well, Bartholomeus, how are you?

BART II: [*to* BART III] Well, Bartholomeus, how are you?

BART I: [*to* BART III] Well, Bartholomeus, how are you?

BART III: [*to* BART I] Well, Bartholomeus, how are you? [*To*

IONESCO:] Glad I've found you in! I damned nearly went away, and I'd have been very angry, specially as you haven't a phone... What on earth were you doing?

[*The pace of the actors' delivery should increase.*]

IONESCO: I was working... working... I was writing!

BART III: The new play? Is it ready? I'm waiting for it.

IONESCO: [*sitting down and indicating a chair to* BART III] Sit down. [BART III *sits down by the others, all three in a row.*] Well, I'm working on it, you know. I've got right down to it. It's coming along, but it's not easy. It's got to be perfect, no repetition, no dull passages. I'm always being accused of going round in circles in my plays... so I'm tightening, tightening it up...

BART III: You can read us at least the beginning.

BART II: [*echo*] At least the beginning...

BART I: [*echo*] ... least the beginning...

IONESCO: [*reading*] 'Ionesco is asleep, his head on the table, surrounded with books and manuscripts. The doorbell rings. Ionesco snores. It rings again. Ionesco goes on snoring. Then there is a knocking at the door...'

[*Suddenly there is a real knocking at the door.*]

IONESCO: Yes, just a second!... What's the matter now?

[*Smoothing his untidy hair,* IONESCO *starts making for the door.*]

BART III: Sounds quite interesting... but let's hear the rest...

BART II: [*to* IONESCO] It's very unexpected.

[*Fresh knocking at the door.*]

BART I: [*to the other two*] That's because you weren't here from the start. I know this play a bit better. [*To* IONESCO:] It's a vicious circle.

IONESCO: A vicious circle can have its virtues too!

BART I: So long as you get out of it in time.

IONESCO: Oh, yes, that's true... so long as you get out of it.

BART II: And there's only one way to get out of it, and that's the right way. [*To* BART I:] Isn't it, Dr Bartholomeus? [*Then, to* BART III:] Isn't it, Dr Bartholomeus?

BART III: Perhaps.

BART II: [*to* IONESCO] You can only get out of a vicious circle by enclosing yourself in it. So don't go and open the door or the vicious circle will close in more... on you.

BART I: We've seen it happen before.

BART II: Yes, we've seen it happen before.

IONESCO: I don't understand.

BART III: I don't understand, there's an expression I *do* understand... or at least it's one I *use*.

BART II: [*to* IONESCO] It's easy to see *you*'re not a scholar!

[*Gesture of commiseration from the three* BARTHOLOMEUS.]

BART I [*to* IONESCO]: We'll explain it all to you. Now.

BART II: Well now.

BART III: Let's see.

BART I: Instead of the expression 'get out of', say 'get away from', which means 'alienate yourself', and then you'll understand. For example, you can only alienate yourself from a vicious circle by not escaping from it; whereas you can only escape from it by staying inside. What is inside is experienced from the outside, and what is outside is experienced from the inside. For the more alienated you are...

BART II: ... the more involved you are...

BART I: ... and the more involved you are...

BART II: ... the more alienated you are. It's the electrical shock of alienation, or the Y effect.

BART III: [*aside*] Pure philosophistry! They're both philosophisters!

BART II: [*to* BART I] We understand each other, Maître Bartholomeus. [*To* BART III:] We understand each other, Maître Bartholomeus, although there are still some little points of disagreement...

[*The three* BARTHOLOMEUS *bow to one another*.]

BART I: [*to* IONESCO] That is to say, one is inside when one is outside, outside when one is inside, or popularly speaking, I mean...

BART II: Scientifically...

BART III: Quite simply.

BART I: ... and dialectically speaking, it's called: The Being-In-on-the-Outside-and-Out-on-the-Inside. [*To the other two* BARTHOLOMEUS:] It's also the Being of not-Being and the Not-Being of Being in the Know... [*To* IONESCO:] Have you thought about this question?

IONESCO: Er... a little... vaguely... I haven't exactly gone into it...

BART II: [*to* BART I] Authors aren't here to think, they're here to write what they're told.

IONESCO: I beg your pardon, but I... I find you're expressing yourself in a very contradictory way. I'm all for contradiction, everything is nothing but contradiction, and yet any systematic exposition ought not to... should it... in words, confuse opposites...

BART I: I can see you don't know...

BART II: [*to* BART III] He doesn't appear to know it...

BART III: [*to* BART II] Doesn't know it at all!

BART I: [*to* BART II *and* BART III] Be quiet! [*To* IONESCO:] So you don't know that opposites are identical? Here's an example. When I say that something is truly true, that means that it's falsely false...

BART II: Or just the reverse: if something is falsely false, it's also truly true...

IONESCO: I'd never have thought of that. Oh, how clever you are!

BART I: Yet, on the other hand, you can say that the more truly false something is, the more falsely true it is. And the less truly false it is, the less falsely true. To sum up: the false true is the true false, or the true true is the false false. And so opposites cancel out, *quod erat demonstrandum.*

IONESCO: In such a case, I'm sorry, it seems to me that the false is not the true, the true is not the false, and opposites exclude each other.

BART II: What cheek! He thinks... [*To* BART I *and* BART III:]

... He thinks like a pig!

IONESCO: [*speechless, after a short pause*] Ah yes, yes... I see...

BART II: What do you see?

IONESCO: I see... I'm beginning to see... er... what you mean... I can see a few shadows...

BART III: He's beginning to see the light...

BART II: Do you think his mind's going to thaw?

IONESCO: What, I'm muddling it up... what's true is true and what's false is false...

BART I: Horror! Tautologies! Nothing but tautologies! And every tautology is the expression of wrong thinking!

BART II: It's obviously inconceivable to identify something with itself.

BART III: [*to* BART I] Don't get so worked up. It's not his fault if he doesn't understand. He's an intellectual. A man of the theatre ought to be stupid!

BART II: He hasn't got a people's mind, by that I mean scientific.

BART I: [*to* BART II *and* BART III] His mentality's prehistoric, pithecanthropic, he's the 'missing link'... [*In a whisper:*] I even suspect him of being a bit of a Platonist.

BART III: Oh... how ghastly! A Platonist... what animal's that?

BART II: [*whispering in* BART I'*s ear*] I don't think so. I've still got some faith in him, in spite of everything...

BART I: Well, *I* haven't got much... These prolific poets and playwrights who deliver the goods like hens laying eggs... You can't trust them, can't trust them...

BART III: [*aside*] A Platonist?... Oh yes, it's a kind of platypus!

BART II: But we have to make use of them!

[*The three* BARTHOLOMEUS *whisper in each other's ears.*]

IONESCO: I'd like to know what I'm being accused of!

BART III: [*severely*] Laying eggs!

IONESCO: I'll try not to lay any more...

BART III: You'd better not!

BART I: [*after a confabulation with* BART II, *to* IONESCO] Now listen, Ionesco. Bartholomeus [*Pointing to him.*] Bartholomeus

[*Pointing to* BART II :] and I, we all wish you the best... and we want to do something for you.

IONESCO: Thanks very much...

BART II: We want to teach you.

IONESCO: But I went to school.

BART II: [*to* BART I] That's just what we were afraid of.

BART I: [*to* IONESCO] All the knowledge and science you picked up there was false...

IONESCO: I was very bad at science.

BART III: Well, at least that's something in his favour. [*To the two* BARTHOLOMEUS:] His mind's a blank on that score...

BART II: [*to* BART III] So long as he learnt something else, something else.

IONESCO: I was made to read the works of Aeschylus, Sophocles and Euripides...

BART I: Outdated, outdated, all that! It's dead... of no value at all...

IONESCO: And then... and then... Shakespeare!

BART III: He's not a *French* writer. The others may be, but *he's* a Russian.

BART II: [*to* BART I] We don't blame him for being foreign.

BART III: But I do, I blame him for it. [*Aside :*] I think he was Polish after all.

BART II: [*to* BART III] My dear Maître Bartholomeus, you've every right to blame him, you're a critic ... [*Visibly ill at ease,* IONESCO *mops his brow.*] You can be full of blame, for everything, that's your mission in life.

BART III: [*to* BART II] It's yours too, my dear Bartholomeus. [*To* BART I:] And yours, my dear Bartholomeus.

BART I: [*to* BART II *and* BART III] And yours... and yours...

BART II: [*to* BART III *and* BART I] And yours... and yours...
[*Bows all round.*]

IONESCO: I studied a little Molière too.

BART II: Dreadful, dreadful mistake!

BART I: [*to* BART II] Molière? Do you know?

BART II: [to BART I] An author who wrote about Affected and Learned Ladies...

BART I: [to BART II] If he praised Affected and Learned Ladies he belongs to the Age of Science! He's one of us!

BART II: [to BART I] You're mistaken, my dear Bartholomeus, on the contrary, he held them up to ridicule.

BART I: [horrified, to IONESCO] Disgraceful! Poor man, are those your authors? That explains why you've the mentality of the lower middle class.

BART III: He hasn't been accepted by the commercial theatre yet. That makes him dangerous. [He points his index finger at IONESCO:] And so are you.

IONESCO: Yes... I see... I'm sorry.

BART II: [also pointing his finger at IONESCO] He's a bad writer.

BART I: [doing the same] A reactionary!

BART III: [as before] Ah yes, I remember, he got his inspiration from foreigners, from the Italians.

BART II: [as before] With a bad influence!

IONESCO: [very timidly] As Molière still amuses, I thought he was of universal, of eternal interest.

BART II: Blasphemy!

BART I: Only the ephemeral is of lasting value.

IONESCO: [backing to the right before the pointed fingers of the Doctors] ... Like the provisional... of course... yes, yes...

BART II: If these plays still seem to you to have some value, your deluded senses have led you astray.

BART I: All it means is that Molière failed to express the social gestus of his age.

BART III: [to IONESCO] You hear what these gentlemen are saying?

IONESCO: [with a supreme effort] It's true. I prefer Shakespeare.

BART III: [aside] He's not Polish. I must look him up in Larousse. [He looks in the Petit Larousse.]

BART I: [to IONESCO] What do you find so wonderful about this writer?

IONESCO: [to BART I] I find Shakespeare's very, very...

BART III: [*shutting the dictionary*] Yes, Larousse says he's Polish.

BART II: [*to* IONESCO] What do you find he is?

IONESCO: I found that Shakespeare is... poetic!

BART I: [*perplexed*] Poetic?

BART II: Poetic, poetic?

IONESCO: [*timidly*] Poetic.

BART III: Poetic, poetic, poetic?

IONESCO: Yes, by that I mean that there's poetry in it...

BART III: Jargon! Another piece of jargon.

BART I: But what *is* this poetry?

BART III: [*to* BART I *and* BART II] Good Lord... poetry!...
[*Pursing his lips in scorn.*]

BART II: [*to* BART III] Be quiet! No poetry, please. [*To* BART I:]
Poetry's an enemy of our science!

BART I: [*to* IONESCO] You're steeped in false knowledge.

BART III: He only likes wild and extravagant nonsense.

BART I: [*to* BART II *and* BART III, *indicating* IONESCO] His mind
hasn't been properly trained...

BART II: It's been warped.

BART III: We must straighten it out.

BART II: If we can. [*To* BART III:] But not, my dear Bartholomeus, in the direction you want it to take. We disagree on
several points, as you very well know.

BART I: We'll straighten it first. And once we've got it straight
we'll argue about the direction it's got to take.

[*Short, inaudible confabulation between the three* BARTHOLOMEUS.]

BART III: That's right. We must take the most urgent things first.

BART II: [*to* IONESCO] Can you hear what we say?

IONESCO: [*with a start*] Yes, yes... yes... of course... I'm not
deaf.

BART I: [*to* IONESCO] We're going to ask you a few questions...

IONESCO: A few questions?

BART II: [*to* IONESCO] To find out what you know...

IONESCO: What I know...

BART III: [*to* IONESCO] Straighten your warped knowledge.

IONESCO: Warped, yes...

BART I: [*to* IONESCO] Clear up all the confusion in your mind...

IONESCO: All the confusion in my mind...

BART I: [*to* IONESCO] First of all, do you know what the theatre is?

IONESCO: Er, the theatre is theatre.

BART II: [*to* IONESCO] Quite wrong.

BART I: [*to* IONESCO] Wrong... the theatre is a manifestation of theatricality.

BART III: [*to* BART I *and* BART II] But does he know what theatricality is?

BART I: [*to* BART II *and* BART III] We'll soon find out. [*To* IONESCO:] Define theatricality.

IONESCO: Theatricality... theatricality... is what is theatrical...

BART I: I was afraid of that...

BART II: So was I.

BART III: So was I.

BART I: I was afraid his thinking was tainted. [*To* IONESCO:] You're out of your mind, theatricality is what is anti-theatrical.

BART III: [*to* BART I] I don't quite agree with you there. I believe, my dear Bartholomeus, that theatricality may be... it's not because *he* said it, [*He points to a collapsed* IONESCO.] *he* doesn't know what he's saying, he got it right because he misunderstood... what is theatrical is theatrical...

BART I: Give an example.

IONESCO: Yes, an example!

BART II: [*to* IONESCO] Keep out of this, can't you!

BART III: I can't find an example that springs to mind, but I'm right... All that matters is that I'm always right!

BART II: [*conciliatory, to* BART I] Perhaps one kind of thing that's theatrical is theatrical, while another isn't... it's all a question of knowing which kind...

BART I: But no... but no... [*To* IONESCO:] It's not your turn to speak!

IONESCO: I'm not saying a word.

BART II: [*to* IONESCO] There you are, you see, you *are*...

BART I: [to IONESCO] But no... [To BART II:] You're wrong, my dear Bartholomeus. Phenomenologically speaking theatricality is never theatrical.

BART II: Sorry, sorry, but *theatre* is theatrical...

IONESCO: [*timidly rasing one finger*] I wonder if... I could...

BART I: [to IONESCO] Quiet. [*To* BART III:] You're thinking tautologically! The theatrical resides in the anti-theatrical and vice versa... vice versa... vice versa...

BART II: Veecee-verso... Veecee-verso... Veecee-verso!

BART III: Veecee-verso? Oh not veecee-verso, it's versa-vircee.

BART I: I say vircee-versa.

BART III: I maintain it's versa-vircee!

BART I: Vircee-verso!

BART III: You can't frighten me: versa-vircee.

BART II: [*to the other* BARTHOLOMEUS] Don't argue in front of him... It weakens our academic doctoral authority... [*Indicating* IONESCO:] Don't forget, don't forget we must first straighten him out, then train him straight.

IONESCO: [*who has recovered some of his courage*] Gentlemen, perhaps the theatre is, quite simply, drama, action, action at a given time and place...

BART II: [to BART III *and* BART I] You see! He's already taken advantage of us, because of our quarrels.

BART I: [to IONESCO] What do you know about it?

IONESCO: I believe it... and then Aristotle said it.

BART III: A Levantine!

BART I: Aristotle, Aristotle! What's Aristotle got to do with it?

BART II: To start with, he wasn't the first who said it.

BART I: [to IONESCO] Do you know who said it long before Aristotle? Long before!

BART II: Oh yes... long, long before Aristotle!

IONESCO: I don't know...

BART I: Adamov, Monsieur.

IONESCO: Really?... He said it before... before Aristotle?

BART II: Certainly!

BART III: Yes, that's true, he said it first.

BART II: All Aristotle did was say the same thing in different words.

BART I: Only Adamov has realized his mistake since then!

BART II: And so must Aristotle.

BART I: The theatre, Monsieur, is a lesson about some instructive happening, an event of educational value... We must raise the level of the public...

BART III: We must lower it.

BART I: No, maintain it!

BART II: They should come to the theatre to learn!

BART I: Not laugh!

BART III: Or cry!

BART I: Or forget!

BART II: Or forget themselves!

BART I: Or for exaltation!

BART II: Or for sublimation!

BART I: Or self-identification!

BART III: A playwright should be a schoolteacher...

BART II: That's who we train, we critics and scholars: schoolteachers.

BART III: It's the schoolteacher should train the playwright!

BART I: The public shouldn't enjoy themselves at the theatre!

BART II: Those who enjoy themselves will be punished!

BART III: After all, there's a sensible way of finding entertainment.

BART I: Learning is part of entertainment.

BART III: But the theatre's where you have a good time.

BART II: Boredom is entertainment.

BART III: It's theatre when it's not la-di-da.

BART I: Our kind of entertainment's become an anachronism! We haven't as yet discovered the appropriate recreation for our time.

BART III: I don't belong to my time... what's it matter, let's be zany...

BART I: You're right there... it's amazing how limited the

public is in the way it expresses its feelings...

BART II: Their reactions show little variation.

BART I: I've drawn up a list. And I've noticed the public shows its approval by means of applause.

IONESCO: I've noticed that too.

BART III: That's what theatre is, when you shout: Bravo!

BART II: Or cat-call...

BART I: Or whistle...

IONESCO: It hasn't happened at my plays yet!

BART II: Or stamp their feet.

BART I: Very unusual.

IONESCO: [aside] What else do they want them to do! Hiccup, belch, click their tongues, whoop like Red Indians or break their wind?

BART I: The public's reactions are really very elementary.

BART II: Monotonous, stereotyped...

BART III: The public's too intelligent!

BART II: The public's too stupid!

BART I: Why do they clap their hands, then?

BART II: The Latins called it *plaudere*.

BART I: The Greeks used the verb *Krotein*.

BART II: But why do they tap their feet?

IONESCO: [aside] No one will ever know.

BART I: Is it because a lively emotion provokes irregular motion?

IONESCO: [aside] I've never asked myself that question.

BART I: [to BART III] It must be due to the theatre's social past.

IONESCO: [aside] That must be it.

BART I: If we can't get the public to bring intelligent variation to the expression of their feelings, they'd better stop having any! From now on the public will have to observe the maximum restraint...

BART II: The theatre will be a night school.

BART III: For the dull and the backward!

BART II: A compulsory course.

BART I: With medals and rewards.

BART III: And hot steam baths for their health!

BART I: And a system of punishment.

[IONESCO, *alarmed, is turning his head rapidly from one Doctor to the next, faster and faster.*]

BART II: The theatre's a lesson in things.

BART I: In the scientific theatre the programme-sellers will be prefects.

BART II: Or junior teachers to invigilate at rehearsals.

BART III: No objection to that!

BART II: The director will be the vice-principal.

BART I: No more intervals!

BART II: Just a ten-minute break for recreation!

BART III: Objection to that!

BART II: If any playgoer fails to understand...

BART I: Or wants to leave the room...

BART III: All I say is...

BART I: He must raise his hand...

BART II: And ask permission to go...

BART III: ... that I don't understand a word...

BART I: Every playgoer will be expected to come and see the same play several times and learn it off by heart...

BART II: To understand it properly and each time study a different scene! From a different point of view!

BART III: ... never understood a word!

BART I: Concentrate on a different actor!

BART II: Attain the ultimate interpretation of the work in question...

BART I: Which would be the sum of a whole line of successive and contradictory interpretations...

BART II: ... and so reach a final understanding, which should be simple, multifarious and unique!

BART I: Theatregoers will take notes and be classed in order of merit at the end of the year...

BART III: The last shall be first.

BART II: The lazy shall be failed...

BART III: The loafers rewarded!

BART I: We'll organize holiday shows and summer festivals.

BART II: When the non-scientific public will come back and see the same play again.

BART I: Until they get it into their thick heads and we make scientists of donkeys!

BART III: [to IONESCO, *who has retreated, terrified, into a corner*] You're keeping very quiet?

IONESCO: I... I... I... It's because you...

BART II: Be quiet!

BART III: Say something!

BART I and II: [*to* IONESCO] Speak...

BART III: [*to* IONESCO] Be quiet!

IONESCO: I... I...

BART II: Don't you agree with us?

IONESCO: [*as before*] Oh... no...

BART I: What, no?

IONESCO: I mean... yes... yes...

BART III: Yes what? Have you got reservations?

IONESCO: [*as before*] I mean, yes... yes... yes...

BART II: What does Yes mean?

IONESCO: [*with a great effort*] I agree... yes... all right... I agree to your... enlightening me... there's nothing I want more...

BART I: [*to* BART II] He's making confession of his own ignorance.

BART II: [*to* IONESCO] You admit your mistakes?

IONESCO: [*with an effort*] Why yes, Gentlemen... yes... my ignorance, my mistakes... I'm very sorry... please forgive me... all I ask is to be taught what's right... [*He beats his chest.*] Mea culpa! Mea maxima culpa!

BART III: [*to* BART I *and* II] Is this sincere?

IONESCO: [*with warmth and conviction*] Oh yes... I swear it is!...

BART II: No sinner but should find mercy.

IONESCO: [*overcome*] Oh thank you... thank you... How good you are, Gentlemen!

BART I: [*to* BART II] Don't give way to the temptation of goodness! We'll soon see if he's really sincere.

IONESCO: Oh yes, I am sincere.

BART III: Let him prove it, then, by his works.

BART I: Not by his works.

BART II: His works don't count.

BART I: It's only his theories that count.

BART II: What one *thinks* of one's work.

BART I: For the work in itself...

BART II: Doesn't exist...

BART I: Except in what one says about it...

BART I: In the interpretation you're willing to give it...

BART II: That you impose on the work...

BART I: That you impose on the public.

IONESCO: Very well, Gentlemen, very well, Gentlemen, I agree
with what you say... I tell you again I'll do as you say and I'll
prove it to you.

BART II: [*to* BART I *and* BART III] But we've still got to decide
what we mean by sincerity!

BART I: Which is not what one usually thinks it is!

BART II: What one takes empirically...

BART I: Unscientifically...

BART III: Foolishly...

BART II: ... to be sincerity... For sincerity, in fact, is its
opposite!

BART III: Not always, perhaps!

BART II: More often than not!

BART I: [*to* BART III *and* BART II] *Always*, Gentlemen!... Always,
for to be sincere, you have to be insincere!

BART II: [*to* BART III] The only real sincerity...

BART I: [*to* BART III] ... is when you're double-faced...

BART II: [*to* BART III] And ambiguous.

BART III: [*to* BART I *and* BART II] Gentlemen... allow me, on
this point...

BART I: [*interrupting* BART III] But it's perfectly clear.

BART III: It seems obscure to me.

BART II: It's clear-obscure.

BART I: I'm sorry, it's clear obscurity...

BART III: Forgive me, but clear obscurity is not clear-obscure.

BART II: You're mistaken...

[*While the three Doctors are quarrelling,* IONESCO *withdraws slightly, apparently hoping to be forgotten. Then he tries to escape on tip-toe to the door.*]

BART I: Gentlemen, I maintain that obscurity is clear, just as a lie is truth...

BART II: You mean, just as truth is a lie!

BART III: Not quite to the same extent!

BART II: Yes, exactly the same!

BART III: Not quite.

BART I: Oh yes.

BART II: My dear Bartholomeus...

BART III: No...

BART I: Yes.

BART III: No.

BART I: Yes...

BART II: Yes and no.

BART III: No.

BART I: Yes.

BART II: No and yes.

BART III: No.

BART II: My dear Bartholomeus, there's a subtle distinction there...

BART I: I don't hold with distinctions...

BART III: Neither do I.

BART II: [*to* BART I] You know perfectly well I quite agree with you about general principles... But on this particular point...

BART I: To hell with particular points: mystification is demystification, confession is dissimulation, trust is abuse... abuse of trust.

BART II: That's really profound!

BART III: [*to* BART I] I'd say it was just the opposite.

BART I: Rubbish!... According to you, I suppose dissimulation is confession.

BART III: Obviously!

BART I: [*to* BART III] You're floundering.

BART III: No, I'm not!

BART II: Gentlemen, Gentlemen...

BART I: Yes you are...

BART II: Gentlemen, Gentlemen... *please*, don't start that again. We mustn't set a bad example. United we stand against the foe!

BART I: [*holding his hand out to* BART III] United we stand against the foe!

BART II: United we stand against the foe!

BART III: Very well, united we stand against the foe.

> [*All three stand in a solemn group, giving a triple handshake; then, a moment later, they look at the place where* IONESCO *was and is no more:*]

Where *is* the foe?

BART I: Where *is* the foe?

BART II: Where *is* the foe? [*Catching sight of* IONESCO *near the door:*] Traitor!

BART III: Traitor!

BART I: So you wanted to escape, you were running away?

BART III: [*to* BART I *and* BART II] Shame on him! He deserves hanging!

IONESCO: Oh no... really I don't...

BART I: [*to* IONESCO] What does this mean, then?

BART III: [*to* IONESCO] Why are you over by the door?

IONESCO: It just happened, I swear, it happened quite by chance...

BART III: [*to* IONESCO] You can't deny you left your chair...

IONESCO: No, I can't deny that.

BART II: [*to* IONESCO] Well?

BART III: [*to* IONESCO] Defend yourself...

IONESCO: [*stammering*] I was only going away to find it easier to stay, it was just an escape, or rather an *un*just escape, to prevent me from leaving... [*With greater assurance:*] Yes, I was going away the better to stay...

BART III: [*to* BART I *and* BART II] What do you make of it?

BART II: [*to* BART I *and* BART III] What he says seems sensible enough, it's true the more you stay the more you go away...

BART I: [*to* BART II *and* BART III] And the more you go away the more you stay, it's all in line.

BART II: He sounds dishonest to me, that is to say, dialectically, honest...

BART III: Isn't he trying to pull the wool over our eyes?

BART I: [*to* BART III] He's too stupid for that.

BART II: He wouldn't dare. [*To* IONESCO:] Anyhow don't you move again without our permission! [*To* BART III *and* BART I:] We'll be on the safe side.

[*An old woman's voice behind the door calls out: Ionesco! Monsieur Ionesco!*]

IONESCO: Gentlemen, Gentlemen, please, I must open the door, she's been there a long time!

BART III: Who is it then? Some uninvited guest!

IONESCO: It's the woman next door who does my housework.

BART II: Ionesco, don't move... sit down... be quick about it...

BART III: You've already been told twice before: I shan't say it a third time.

BART II: Do you realize you've got everything to learn from us?

[*Knocking at the door, then you hear: What on earth's the matter with him! IONESCO throws worried glances at the door, he'd like to open it.*]

IONESCO: I admit that! Everything, my dear Maîtres, everything...

BART II: All about theatricality?

IONESCO: Yes.

BART I: All about costumology?

IONESCO: All about costu... what?

BART I: [*to* BART II] Poor devil! He doesn't know what costumology is! [*To* IONESCO:] You'll learn!

IONESCO: I'll learn...

BART II: All about historicization and decorology...

IONESCO: I'll do the best I can!

BART III: You must also know about the psychology of the audience, about audienco-psychology! Up to now you've been writing plays without thinking about them...

IONESCO: I'll think about them from now on, I'll think about them day and night!

BART I: Promise?

IONESCO: Promise, I swear!

BART III: I shan't say it a third time.

IONESCO: [*scared*] Oh no... There's no need, really there isn't!

BART I: We'll give you the basic elements of this new science. The theory first, the practice later.

BART III: Just listen to us for now and take notes!

IONESCO: Yes... yes... I'll take some notes.

[*Sitting at his study table, he searches among his numerous exercise books, with difficulty finds a blank page and feverishly settles himself down, pencil in hand; meanwhile the Doctors are talking amongst themselves.*]

BART III: What shall we start with?

BART II: [*to* BART I] Start, dear colleague, if you like, yourself, with costumology...

BART I: [*to* BART II] Start, dear colleague, yourself, with theatricology...

BART I and BART II: [*to* BART III] Start, if you like, yourself, with audienco-psychology...

BART III: [*to* BART I *and* BART II] After you, Gentlemen... Make a... methodical start.

[*Knocking at the door.*]

WOMAN'S VOICE: Monsieur! Ah!... He's locked himself in... What's he doing? I haven't the time to...

[IONESCO *is worried, makes a gesture towards the door, opens his mouth, but dares not open the door.*]

BART I: [*to* BART II] After you...

BART II: [*to* BART I] I'll do no such thing...

BART III: Neither shall I... I'd never forgive myself.

BART II: [*to* BART I] It would be lacking in courtesy...

[*Knocking at the door. The Woman's voice: Hey! You there, inside!*]

BART I: [*to* BART II] I should be wanting in manners...

BART II: [*to* BART III] After you...

BART III: [*to* BART I] You can't really mean it...

BART I: [*to* BART II] Neither can you... After you...

[*Then suddenly, turning to face* IONESCO, *who is gazing at the door, looking more and more worried, the three* BARTHOLOMEUS *all together and at precisely the same moment rush into the following :*]

BART I: ⎫ Every playwright's ABC of theatricology...

BART II: ⎬ Every playwright's ABC of costumology...

BART III: ⎭ Every playwright's ABC of audiencology...

ALL THREE: ... decorology!

IONESCO: [*alarmed*] Gentlemen, Gentlemen...

BART I: [*to* BART II *and* BART III] So sorry!

BART II: [*to* BART I *and* BART III] So sorry!

BART III: [*to* BART I *and* BART II] So sorry!

IONESCO: Please don't apologize!

[*Then, suddenly as before, while* BART I *and* BART III *fall over each other in exchanging compliments and apologies behind* BART II's *back, the latter, standing alone to face* IONESCO, *addresses him in a loud voice :*]

BART II: Monsieur. [IONESCO *stands up.*] Sit down. [IONESCO *sits down again. To the two* BARTHOLOMEUS, *who have not stopped being silently polite to each other :*] Be quiet, Gentlemen.

[BART I *and* BART III *take up a position on each side of* BART II *and slightly to the rear, showing true doctoral deference.*]

BART II: [*to* IONESCO] You're seriously ill, my dear chap...

[*The other two* BARTHOLOMEUS *gravely nod approval.*]

IONESCO: [*very frightened*] Why, what's the matter with me?

BART II: Don't interrupt! Even if you are no longer ignorant of your own ignorance, you still seem to ignore the fact that an ignorant man is seriously ill...

IONESCO: [*relieved*] Oh... so it's not so bad as I thought! I feared the worst!

BART III: [*to* BART I] What ignorance!

BART I: [*to* BART III] A really sick man!

BART II: [*to* BART I *and* BART III] *I'm* doing the talking. That's what we agreed. [*To* IONESCO:] The disease of the ignorant man is ignorance. As you are an ignorant man, you're suffering from ignorance. And I'll prove it to you! [*With great satisfaction to the other two* BARTHOLOMEUS:] I'll prove it to him. [*To* IONESCO:] Do you know why plays are written?

IONESCO: I don't know how to answer that. Let me think.

BART II: [*to* IONESCO] My dear chap, plays are written to be performed, to be seen and heard by the public in a playhouse, like this one for example...

BART I: Well said, my dear Bartholomeus, well said, a very profound thought...

IONESCO: [*quite lost*] I don't know whether... whether it's profound, but it's certainly correct. Why, even I, in my ignorance, I thought *I* knew that.

BART II: But that's not all. A theatrical performance brings the theatre into being. A text is made to be spoken, and who, do you think, should speak it?... Actors, my dear fellow, actors. To put the idea succinctly, you might say that performance is the breath of life to the theatre!

IONESCO: True. Yes, that's very true.

BART I: [*to* IONESCO, *severely*] It isn't true, it's more than true, it's erudite, it's scientific!

BART III: Plays are made to be performed before an audience!

BART II: You can't say it too often: there's no theatre without an audience!

BART I: And no theatre without a stage, or at least without boards!

BART II: No stage without decor, no admission without ticket, no box office without attendant, male or female...

BART III: No stage without actor.

VOICE: [*from outside the door*] Now look here, Monsieur Ionesco, I've been here for an hour and I've got other things to do. [*To someone else outside:*] I think they're having a fight in there, perhaps they'll hurt him, should I call the police?

ONESCO: [*directing his words to the door*] I'm coming, Marie, I'll open the door.. don't call the police... [*To the three Doctors:*] Gentlemen, I'm very sorry, my room's got to be tidied up a bit, you can see the state it's in, the cleaner's waiting...

BART I: Don't worry your head about that!

IONESCO: It's so dirty.

BART II: That's not important!

MARIE'S VOICE: [*from behind the door*] If you don't open up, I'll call the concierge to break the door down.

IONESCO: [*directing his voice to the door*] I'm coming... I'm coming... [*To the Doctors:*] Gentlemen, Doctors, dear Maîtres, you've just said, haven't you, so wisely and so brilliantly explained that there's no theatre without an audience... then why not let Marie in... [*He makes for the door.*]

BART I: [*to* IONESCO] One second, wait until I give the order.

IONESCO: [*to the door*] Just a minute, I'm waiting for the order. [*The Doctors whisper together, with much gesticulation, in conference.* IONESCO *is like a cat on hot bricks.*]

BART II: I think he'd better open it.

BART I: She might have the whole district up in arms.

BART III: We don't want any trouble with the police...

BART I: [*to* IONESCO] Go and open it, then... [IONESCO *starts moving.*] Wait, just a minute!... We can't let the audience in just like that. We've got to arrange the set, historicize it.

BART II: Let's arrange the set.

BART I: Open the treatise of the great Dr Bertholus.

IONESCO: [*shouting to the door*] Be patient, Marie, just a little longer, they're getting the set ready.

MARIE: What's that?

IONESCO: The set. It won't be long!

[*Meanwhile the Doctors have consulted Bertholus' book and are fetching and arranging the props.*]

IONESCO: [*to the Doctors*] Hurry up. Gentlemen... please hurry up!

BART I: [*reading from the treatise*] It is essential to put up a sign to indicate the action...

[*At the front of one side of the stage* BART III *puts up a sign which reads:* A PLAYWRIGHT'S EDUCATION. IONESCO *goes up to it to read what is written and makes a gesture of despair.*]

BART I: [*reading*] ... to summarize it and draw the public's attention to the fundamental epic attitude enshrined in each tableau...

[*At the opposite side of the stage* BART II *places another sign on which is written:* STYLISED REALISM. IONESCO *crosses over to read once more what is written and makes the same gesture of despair.*]

BART I: [*his nose in the treatise*]... To make it clear that the place is not a real one...

[BART II *abruptly sweeps all the books and papers from the table and hangs up a sign which reads:* FALSE TABLE. *Same reaction from* IONESCO.]

IONESCO: My manuscripts!! [*He tears at his hair.*]

BART I: [*his nose still in the treatise*]... that it makes no claim at all to represent a real place...

[*At the back of the stage* BART II *puts up a larger sign on which is written:* FALSE PLACE. *Same reaction from* IONESCO *who, his back to the audience, raises his arms in the air.*]

BART I: [*to* IONESCO] Keep still, can't you, what's wrong with you? Instead of running wild like that, you'd far better help us with the props, which characterize the historical situation we're expected to pass judgment on.

[*Meanwhile, on an old armchair and on one of the chairs* BART I *and* BART II *place two signs which read*: FAKE.]

BART III: [*aside*] Fake is the concrete convention!

BART II: [*aside*] Fake is the abstract convention!

IONESCO: [*to* BART I] Yes, all right... all right...

[*He runs wildly from one to the other.*]

BART I: [*reading*] Above all one must historicize.

[BART II *and* BART III *pull down a picture hanging on the back wall in order to put signs up in its place.* BART II's *sign reads:* BRECHT TIME, BART III's *sign reads:* BERNSTEIN TIME.]

BART II: [*to* BART III] Oh no, you've got the wrong period...

BART III: [*to* BART II] You've got the wrong period...

BART II: [*to* BART III] I'm very sorry but...

BART III: [*to* BART II] You're quite mistaken...

BART I: [*interrupting his work and turning round*] That's enough... come on now... Can't you agree?

BART III: I'm for Bernstein!

BART II: I'm for Brecht!

[*In their excitement the three* BARTHOLOMEUS *upset the furniture and other objects, while* IONESCO *tries despairingly and in vain to put everything back in place.*]

BART I: Gentlemen, Gentlemen...

BART III: Bernstein is great! I'll have no one but Bernstein!...

BART II: Brecht is the only god for me. I am his prophet!

[BART II *and* BART III *each brandishes his sign.*]

BART II and BART III: Brecht, Bernstein, Bernstein, Brecht!!!

[BART I *takes another sign, on which the words:* THE B CENTURY *are written in enormous letters. He fixes it in the middle.*]

BART I: There you are!

[BART II *and* BART III *go and fix their signs in place, one in each opposite corner of the stage.*]

IONESCO: [*looking at the sign: The B Century*] It's all the same to me.

BART I: [*to* BART II *and* BART III] That should settle the argument... Critics must stand together.

IONESCO: I like it better when they quarrel!

[BART II *and* BART III *contemplate the sign: The B Century.*]

BART II: [*Pointing to the sign*] B, that definitely means Brecht.

BART III: B, that definitely means Bernstein.

BART I: [*to the other two*] You're both right...

BART II: [*to* BART III] What did I tell you?

MARIE's VOICE: Well, what's up now? I'm waiting...

BART III: [*to* BART II] What did I tell you?

IONESCO: Do you think this time I could open the door?

BART I: [*to* BART II] Between ourselves, it means the century of Brecht, not Bernstein... [*To* BART III:] Between ourselves, it means Bernstein, an improved version, modernized and alienated...

BART III: [*to* BART I] What do you mean by that?

BART I: [*to* BART III] It's Bernstein just the same, still Bernstein, don't worry... [*He winks at* BART II.]

IONESCO: May I open the door?...

[*The three* BARTHOLOMEUS *turn together to face* IONESCO *again.*]

BART I: Yes, but you can't go like that...

BART II: Not like that...

BART III: Not in the state you're in...

IONESCO: What state am I in?

[*The three* BARTHOLOMEUS *inspect* IONESCO *from head to foot. They exchange looks, wagging their chins.*]

MARIE's VOICE: There are limits, you know. [*Banging on the door.*]

BART I: [*to* BART II] Look... look at the way he's dressed...

BART II: It's incredible!

BART III: Such a mess!

IONESCO: But what's the matter with me then?

BART I: Ionesco, do you know why we wear costume?

[*The three Doctors show their costumes.*]

IONESCO: Why you're wearing costume?

BART I: Because, after all, actors and actresses can't go naked onto the stage.

IONESCO: Yes, I half thought...

BART III: [*aside*] And yet even nudity is a costume, say, at the Folies-Bergères!

BART II: [*to* IONESCO] If doctors of medicine care for the body's ailments, and priests the ailments of the soul, and theatricologists the ailments of the theatre, costumologists have a special care of the ailments of costume: they are costumological doctors.

[BART II *and* BART III *sound* IONESCO's *clothes.*]

BART II: Everything is clothed...

IONESCO: [*who struggles while* BART II *and* BART III *twist him round about*] Gentlemen... Gentlemen...

BART III: Everything is clothed. The trees...

BART I: The animals, with their fur.

BART II: ... The earth, with its crust...

BART I: The stars... fire, water and wind...

IONESCO: I don't understand.

BART I: We children of the scientific age, one day we'll learn how to distinguish the form of fire from its content.

BART III: The form of wind...

BART II: ... from the content of wind...

BART I: The form of water...

BART II: ... from the content of water...

BART I: The very walnut is clothed in its shell, which protects it and alienates...

BART III: [*to* IONESCO] Be a walnut!

BART II: We'll be nutologists...

BART I: Everything, everything is clothed! Costumology in fact is a veritable cosmology...

MARIE: [*outside*] What do you take me for?

BART II: ... for by restricting the word, you widen the notion...

BART I: Costumology is also a moral science: costume must not be egocentric.

BART II: We know the whole pathology of costume.

BART III: Your costume is seriously ill... It's got to be cured...

IONESCO: It's true... it is a little worn... and moth-eaten...
I admit.

BART III: [*smiling at* IONESCO's *naivety*] *That's* not what we
mean...

BART II: Your costume ought to be costumic, and if it isn't it's in
that sense that it's ill!

BART I: You're not dressed like an author of our time... [*To*
BART II *and* BART III:] Let's dress him!

BART II and BART III: Yes, yes, let's dress him!

BART I: A man is nothing without his clothes. Is a naked man
really clothed? I dare maintain he is *not*.

[BART II *and* BART III *have been removing from the startled*
IONESCO *his jacket, tie and shoes, which they promptly put back*
exactly as before. BART II *and* BART III *perform this task while*
BART I *perorates.*]

BART I: Clothing is an investiture...

IONESCO: I can see it's an investment.

BART III: It's also a little investition.

BART I: There are, as you've seen, a few simple little rules for
telling whether a costume is ill or well... Yours is suffering
from hypertrophy of the historical function... It's veridical...

BART II: And it shouldn't be...

BART I: Your costume is just an alibi. It's shirking its responsibility!

IONESCO: I've always dressed like this!

BART I: It's an end in itself.

BART II: It's no connection with your plays... or it's got too
much.

BART I: It ought to be, without being, the costume of an author
of our time...

BART II: It ought to be a sign.

BART III: Costume has its systematical side.

BART I: Your costume is suffering from faulty nutrition...

BART II: It's over-nourished...

BART III: It's under-nourished...

BART II: After all, it doesn't have to be destitute!

BART I: At least, it isn't beautiful! It's not suffering from any aesthetic disease...

BART II: Your costume must undergo a careful and exhaustive course of treatment.

[*An attempt is made to lower* IONESCO's *trousers. He protests.*]

IONESCO: Gentlemen... it's not decent...

BART I: Your costume ought to tear at the heart!

IONESCO: Don't tear it... I haven't got another... It really is the only one...

[*Another pair of trousers is put on over* IONESCO's *pair.*]

BART I: And now for the system of signs, put his badges on...

[BART II *puts a sign on* IONESCO, *who is at this moment with his back to the audience. On it is the word:* POET.]

IONESCO: [*snivelling*] Please, Gentlemen, please. I don't feel I want to write any more at all!

BART III: Be quiet!

BART I: You were a free agent when you committed yourself.

[BART II *puts over his chest another sign, which is not yet visible.* BART III *puts a dunce's cap on his head.*]

BART I: [*to* IONESCO] You'll never escape again now...

[*They turn* IONESCO *round to face the audience. The word* SCIENTIST *is written on the sign over his chest.* IONESCO *grows more and more tearful.*]

BART II: [*to the other two*] We've made something of him, anyhow.

BART I: Now he belongs to us. We've historicized his costume!

[IONESCO *drops down at his table in the same position he had at the start. They raise him up, he falls forward, they raise him up again.*]

BART II: Not completely yet...

BART III: He's coming along, anyway!

BART II: We've still got to teach him to write!

BART III: In the way we want.

BART I: In the state he's in, it's plain sailing...

BART III: It'll be a piece of cake!

BART I: [*to* IONESCO] Now you're presentable, you can let the audience in.

IONESCO: [*at the door, which is still being thumped, in a pitiful voice*] I'm ready, Marie, I'm coming.

BART I: [*looking round him with satisfaction*] It's a regular laboratory!

BART II: We've done a good job of work.

BART II: We're not doctors for nothing.

[*The Woman's voice is still heard behind the door: Monsieur, Monsieur Ionesco!*]

BART I: [*to* IONESCO] Open it.

BART II: [*to* IONESCO] We'll let you.

BART III: [*to* IONESCO] Open it.

MARIE's VOICE: Are you still there?

IONESCO: [*pitiful as ever*] Yes... just a second... What's the matter now?

[*He stands up and takes a step to the door.*]

BART I [*to* IONESCO]: Be careful now, when you go and open it, to play the scene according to the theory of alienation.

BART III: I shan't tell you a fourth time.

IONESCO: [*in the same tone as before*] How do I do it?...

BART II: Without any self-identification. You've always made the mistake of being yourself.

IONESCO: Who else could I possibly be?

BART II: Alienate yourself.

IONESCO: [*almost blubbing*] But how do I do it?

BART III: It's perfectly simple...

BART I: Watch yourself acting... Be Ionesco not being Ionesco!

BART II: Look at yourself with one eye, listen to yourself with the other!

IONESCO: I can't... I can't...

BART I: Why don't you squint, then, squint!...

[IONESCO *squints.*]

BART III: That's the idea. [*To* BART I:] Well done, Bartholomeus!

BART II: [*to* BART I] Well done, Bartholomeus!

BART I: [to IONESCO] Now move to the door...

[IONESCO *says no more. He moves to the door like a sleepwalker.*]

BART III: [to BART I] Not like that!

BART I: [to IONESCO] Move forward one step!...

BART II: [to IONESCO] While you move two back!...

BART I: One step forward! [IONESCO *moves*].

BART II: Two steps back!... [IONESCO *moves*].

BART III: I shan't tell you a fifth time!

BART I: One step forward...

BART II: Two steps back...

BART III: That's it.

BART II: That's it... He's alienated himself! He's done it!

[IONESCO *should arrive right back at the opposite side to the door*].

BART I: [to IONESCO] Now... dance...

BART II: ... sing... talk...

IONESCO: [*gambols about on the same spot and brays*] Hee... haw... hee... haw... hee... haw...

BART I: Write!

IONESCO: Hee... haw...

BART II: Write harder!!

IONESCO: Hee... haw...

BART II: And scientifically!!!

IONESCO: [*modulating his braying*] Hee... haw... hee... haw...

BART I, II and III: [*together*] Write! Write!! Write!!! Write!!!!

IONESCO: Hee... haw... hee... haw... hee... haw...

BART I, II, III and IONESCO: [*together*] Hee! Haw! Hee! Haw! Hee! Haw!

MARIE'S VOICE: They're going to kill him! I'll break the door down!

[*Meanwhile the three* BARTHOLOMEUS *have donned dunce's caps too. While the four characters on the stage go on braying and gambolling about, the door flies open or falls in with a crash.* MARIE *comes in, broom in hand.*]

MARIE: What's all this about? A circus act?

BART I: Stop!... Here's the audience!

[*Stillness falls. The three* BARTHOLOMEUS *may or may not remove their dunce's caps, but* IONESCO *in any case keeps his.*]

MARIE: Well, so that's what you call your 'set'? You've set everything upside down! How can I start cleaning your room now?... Monsieur Ionesco's untidy enough at the best of times, he didn't need you to help him! What have you got the poor man in this state for? And what are you doing, Messieurs, dressed up like that?

BART I: Madame, we'll explain everything...

MARIE: [*pointing to the signs*] You can start by clearing all that away!

BART II: Don't touch them, whatever you do!

MARIE: [*threateningly*] And why shouldn't I?

BART III: It's for you... we've been working for you, for the general public!

MARIE: [*pointing to* IONESCO] This isn't our carnival time!
[*She moves to* IONESCO.]

BART III: Don't go near him or I'll bite!

MARIE: I'm not afraid of you! Just you try, you little mongrel!
[*She turns on* BART III, *broom at the ready.*]

BART III: [*recoiling*] It was only a manner of speaking!

IONESCO: [*to* MARIE] Let me keep my distance... fifteen feet away from the audience.

MARIE: [*to* IONESCO] They've been having you on a piece of string! And you've let them get away with it... [*She goes up to* IONESCO *and turns him this way and that.*] A dunce's cap!.. Poet... Scientist... You don't think that's clever, do you? They're making a fool of you!

IONESCO: Marie, you don't understand, these Gentlemen have given me a costumical costume and signalectical signs... These Gentlemen are learned doctors...

MARIE: Doctors? What sort of illness do *they* cure?

IONESCO: Yes, doctors... theatricologists, costumologists... they cure costume diseases... My costume was very ill!

MARIE: That's a funny thing to cure! Why didn't you send it to the cleaner's?

IONESCO: They're quite right, Marie, you don't understand, they're very clever scientists...

BART II: Listen to us, Madame!

MARIE: Just a minute!...

[*She goes up to* IONESCO *and starts removing his signs and accoutrements.*]

MARIE: [*to* IONESCO, *who is resisting*] Come along, come on now... Let me put you back straight...

BART I: Madame, Madame... You really don't understand...

IONESCO: [*to* MARIE] They cure the theatre's ailments too.

MARIE: They ought to cure themselves...

IONESCO: They're great psychologists and sociologists!

BART II: [*to* MARIE] You hear what he says! He's saying it himself!

MARIE: That's because you've got him all tied up, he's lost his mind!

BART III: [*to* MARIE, *who is removing the props*] Leave them alone, can't you!

MARIE: I'll say I will! You needn't think *I'll* take any notice of you!... You'd better look out, if *I* lose my temper!

[*She lifts her broom and swings it round. The Doctors take refuge in the corners of the stage.*]

IONESCO: [*intervening*] Don't you hurt my doctors!

[MARIE *makes for the Doctors with her broom, after turning her sleeves up for action. The Doctors try to protect themselves from the blows to come.*]

BART II: [*to* MARIE] Wait at least until we've explained...

MARIE: Explained what?

IONESCO: Marie, I know now what function costume has...

[*Reciting:*] In the theatre costume should link the content of the play to its externality.

MARIE: So you wrote a play which had an ordinary fireman in it...*

BART III: [*reacting, shocked*] An ordinary fireman?

---

* A reference to the character of the Fireman in Ionesco's *La Cantatrice Chauve*. The word for Fireman also provides a pun, which has been lost in translation. Tr.

IONESCO: [*to* BART III] Any reference to any character, living or dead, in one of my plays is purely coincidental.

MARIE: [*to* IONESCO] An ordinary fireman, yes, and on his head you put a fireman's helmet, a helmet, mind, and not a bride's veil... And so you really linked the content of your play with its externality!...

BART II: [*who has recovered some of his assurance*] Yes, you wrote in prose and never knew it!

IONESCO: That's what they're here to teach me!

MARIE: Oh, I'm sorry, Monsieur, but you really are ill! [*She slaps* IONESCO *twice in the face.*]

IONESCO: Where am I?

MARIE: You were hypnotized. That'll wake you up.
   [*Dazed,* IONESCO *looks about him, pinches himself, takes off his dunce's cap etc.*]

MARIE: [*to* IONESCO] They've got nothing to teach you!... these wretched doctors have no business giving you advice, it's they who ought to take lessons in drama.

IONESCO: [*to* MARIE] You really think so?

MARIE: [*to* IONESCO] I should say... of course they ought... You're a great big baby!

BART I: [*indignantly*] What's that? What's that? And what about theatricology?

MARIE: [*pushing the Doctors towards the door*] We couldn't care less. [*Quite ferociously following her attack right up to the door.*] You can get rid of all that rubbish!

BART II: And what about audienco-psycho-sociology!

MARIE: Scram!

BART III: Do you know who I am?

MARIE: Vamoose!

BART II: And decorology!

IONESCO: [*rather frightened*] Marie... Marie... Go easy... They'll tear me to pieces in their columns...

MARIE: [*still pushing the three Doctors out and bundling more props into their arms*] Don't be afraid of them, pack of good-for-nothings! [*To the Doctors*:] And take this away with you too...

BART I: [*at the door*] And the science of sciences, costumology?

BART II: [*to* BART I, *recoiling back to the door with the others*] Oh no, not costumology, costumitude!

BART I: [*to* BART II] What do you mean by that?

BART II: I'm a costumitudist, I study the essence of costume.

BART I: No such thing as the essence of costume! Costume's created by costumology...

BART II: It's exactly the opposite!

BART I: So you're an essentialist, then!

BART II: So you're a phenomenalist!

[BART I *and* BART II *come to blows.*]

BART III: [*to* BART I *and* BART II] It's all your fault! Filiburstering philosophisters! Snooty snobs!

BART I: [*to* BART III] Snob yourself!

BART II: [*to* BART III] Commercial hack!

BART III: A snob... I may be... but I'm a well-bred snob!...

BART II: [*to* BART III] Philistine!

BART I: [*to* BART III] You're a silly sot!

BART III: And proud of it!

BART II: [*to* BART III] Boar!

BART I: [*to* BART III] Pig!

BART III: [*to* BART II] Swine!

BART I: [*to* BART II *and* BART III] Hogsheads!⋆

IONESCO: Gentlemen, *please!*

EACH BART to the OTHER TWO: Phoneys! Phoneys! Phoneys!

MARIE: [*to the Doctors*] Go and fight outside!

IONESCO: Marie, a little less violence!

MARIE: [*to* IONESCO] But I tell you they're nothing to be afraid of! [*To the Doctors*:] Out! out! out!

IONESCO: Gentlemen, don't get too excited... don't get so angry! [*The Doctors go out and* MARIE *pushing them. From the wings can be heard cries of:* 'Costumology, costumitude, theatricology, psycho-audiencology... cology... cology.' IONESCO, *who is not exactly calm, stops suddenly next to the door. Then, while you*

⋆ The sequence in the original is 'Calf! Cow! Pig! Brood!' a famous sequence from La Fontaine's fable 'La Laitière et le pot au lait'. Tr.

can still hear 'cology... cology... cology...', he turns round, cups his hand to his ear and listens to the noise dying away. He walks quietly to the table, sits down with assurance and looks again towards the door:] Right! Come on now!... That's enough! The play is over... Back on stage! [*The muffled sounds fom the wings stop abruptly. Then, one by one, the three* BARTHOLOMEUS *come on and line up at the back of the stage behind* IONESCO, *who stands up and says:*] Ladies and Gentlemen...

MARIE: [*who now comes on with a glass and a jug of water*] Just a minute... I expect you're thirsty...

[*She pours some water into the glass.* IONESCO *picks it up and drinks it.*]

IONESCO: Thank you, Marie... [*Then, to the audience:*] Ladies and Gentlemen... [*He takes a paper from his pocket and puts on his spectacles.*] Ladies and Gentlemen, the text you have just heard was very largely taken from the writings of the doctors with me here. If you have been bored, I can hardly be held responsible; if you have been amused, I can claim no credit. The weaker lines and the obvious dramatic tricks are my own. Bartholomeus [*Pointing to* BART I:] is a pedant. Bartholomeus [*Pointing to* BART II:] is also a pedant. [*He hesitates.*] Bartholomeus [*Pointing to* BART III:] is an unpedantic fool. I blame these doctors for discovering elementary truths and dressing them up in exaggerated language so that these elementary truths appear to have gone mad. These truths, however, like all truths, even elementary ones, are open to argument. They become dangerous when they take on the appearance of infallible dogma, and when in their name scholars and critics claim to reject other truths and govern artistic creation even to the point of tyranny. The critic should describe, and not prescribe. Our learned doctors, as Marie has just told you, have everything to learn and nothing to teach, for the creative artist himself is the only reliable witness of his times, he discovers them in himself, it is he alone, mysteriously and in perfect freedom, who can express his day and age. Constraint and control—the history of literature is there to prove it—falsify this evidence and distort it by pushing it [*Gesture to the right.*] in one direction [*Gesture to the left.*] or the other. I distrust the truisms [*Gesture to the right.*] of one side as much [*Gesture to the left.*] as of the other. If however we admit that the critic clearly has the right to exercise his judgment, he should only judge a work on its own terms, according to the laws that govern artistic expression, the mythological structure of each work, and so penetrate each new universe afresh: we don't bring chemistry into music, we don't judge biology according to the criteria of painting or architecture, and astronomy is kept apart from political economy and sociology; if Anabaptists, for example, want to find in a play the illustration of their Anabaptist beliefs, they are free to do so; but when they claim that their Anabaptist faith overrides all and try to convert us, then I oppose them. For my part I believe sincerely in the poverty of the poor, I deplore it, but it is true and can serve as material for the theatre; I also believe in the grave cares and anxieties that may beset the rich; but in my case it is neither from the wretchedness of the poor nor the unhappiness of the rich that I draw the substance of my drama. For me, the theatre is the projection onto the stage of the world within: it is in my dreams, my anguish, my dark desires, my inner contradictions that I reserve the right to find the stuff of my plays. As I am not alone in the world, as each one of us, in the depths of his being, is at the same time everyone else, my dreams and desires, my anguish and my obsessions do not belong to myself alone; they are a part of the heritage of my ancestors, a very ancient deposit to which all mankind may lay claim. It is this which, surpassing the superficial diversity of men, brings them together and constitutes our deepest fellowship, a universal language. [MARIE *takes one of the Doctor's gowns and moves nearer* IONESCO, *who is sounding more and more pedantic.*] It is these hidden desires, these dreams, these secret conflicts which are the source of all our actions and of the reality of history. [IONESCO *is working himself up into an almost aggressive state, very solemn and very ridiculous, accelerating his delivery*:] You see, Ladies and Gentlemen, I believe the language of modern music and painting, as well as the language of physics and higher mathematics and the very essence of history itself are well in advance of the language of the philosophers, who, far behind, painfully struggle to keep up... Scholars are always behind the times, because, as we are told by the eminent Bavarian Steiffenbach and his American disciple Johnson... [MARIE, *who has come right up to* IONESCO *during the last sentence, suddenly throws the gown over his shoulders.*] But... what are you doing, Marie, what are you doing?

BART I: Are you by any chance taking yourself seriously, Ionesco?

IONESCO: Taking myself seriously? No... yes... I mean no...

BART III: It's your turn now to turn academic!

BART I: To be or not to be a doctor, you know, it's the same thing!

BART II: You hate us to give you lessons and now *you* want to give *us* one...

BART I: You've fallen into your own trap.

IONESCO: Oh... this is all very upsetting.

MARIE: One swallow doesn't make a summer.

IONESCO: I'm sorry, I won't do it again, this is the exception...

MARIE: Not the rule!

CURTAIN

Paris 1955

MAID TO MARRY

First produced in Paris by Jacques Polieri at the Théâtre de la Huchette, the 1st September, 1953.

CHARACTERS:

    THE GENTLEMAN
    THE LADY
    THE GENTLEMAID

The LADY is wearing a flowered hat with a big hatpin, a long dress and a short tight-fitting purple jacket. She is carrying a handbag.
The GENTLEMAN has a frock-coat, a high stiff collar and stiff cuffs, a black cravat and a white beard.
They are sitting on a bench in a public park.

LADY: My daughter, let me tell you, was quite brilliant in her studies.

GENTLEMAN: I didn't know, but I'm not surprised. I knew she had plenty of pluck.

LADY: *I've* had no cause to complain, like so many parents. She's always given us perfect satisfaction.

GENTLEMAN: The credit is all yours. You brought her up properly. The model child is very rare, especially nowadays.

LADY: How right you are!...

GENTLEMAN: In my time children were far more obedient, more attached to their parents. They understood the sacrifices they make, their material problems and their difficulties... though from some points of view it's better for them not to.

LADY: I agree!... They were also far more...

GENTLEMAN: They were far more numerous.

LADY: Indeed they were. It seems the birth-rate's falling in France.

GENTLEMAN: It has its ups and downs. Just now it rather shows a tendency to rise again. But we can hardly make up for the lean years!...

LADY: I should say not indeed, you're certainly right there! Just imagine!

GENTLEMAN: What can you expect? It's not easy to bring children up at the present time!...

LADY: Indeed it's not! You don't have to tell *me* that! It's costing more and more to keep alive! And think of all the things they need! What is there they *don't* want?

GENTLEMAN: What's it all leading to?... Today human life is the only thing that's cheap!

LADY: Oh... I *do* so agree with that!... Now that's *very* true... You're *perfectly* right there...

GENTLEMAN: There are earthquakes, accidents, cars and all sorts of other vehicles like aeroplanes, social sickness, voluntary suicide, the atom bomb...

LADY: Oh, *that thing*!... It appears it's changed the weather for us! We don't know where we are with our seasons now, it's upset everything!... And if only that was all... but look, listen, do you know what I've heard people say?...

GENTLEMAN: Oh!... They say so many things! If you had to believe everything you hear!

LADY: That's true of course... There'd be no end to it, indeed there wouldn't!... The papers too, there's a pack of lies for you, lies, all lies!...

GENTLEMAN: Do as I do, Madame, trust nobody, believe in nothing, don't let them stuff your brain with rubbish!...

LADY: I agree. You're better off without. Indeed you are. You've got *your* head screwed on all right. You really have.

GENTLEMAN: Oh, I just *use* mine, that's all!

LADY: You're right there!... But you can't say the same of everyone...

GENTLEMAN: Nowadays you see, Madame, with all our amusements, entertainment and excitement, the cinema, income tax, gramophone record libraries, telephone, radio, air travel, big department stores...

LADY: Ah yes, now you've *said* it!

GENTELEMAN: The prisons, the Grands Boulevards, Social Security, and all that...

LADY: How right you are...

GENTLEMAN: All these things that make the charm of modern life have changed men and women, changed them to such a point that they're unrecognizable!...

LADY: Not changed them for the better either, *now* you've said it.

GENTLEMAN: And yet we can't deny progress, when we see it progressing every day...

LADY: How right you are...

GENTLEMAN: ... in technology, applied science, mechanics, literature and art...

LADY: Of course. We must be fair. It isn't nice to be *un*fair.

GENTLEMAN: You could even go so far as to say that civilization's constantly developing, and in the right direction, thanks to the united efforts of all the nations...

LADY: Perfectly true. I was just about to say the same thing.

GENTLEMAN: We've come a long way since the days of our ancestors, who used to live in caves and gobble each other up and feed on sheepskins!... What a long way we've come!

LADY: Yes, we have, haven't we?... And central heating, Monsieur, what about central heating? Did they have that in their caves?

GENTLEMAN: Well now, dear lady, when I was a small child...

LADY: Such a pretty age!

GENTLEMAN: ... I used to live in the country. I remember it was still the sun that kept us warm, winter and summer alike. We used to light our homes with oil—it's true it wasn't so dear in those days—and sometimes even with candles!...

LADY: That happens even today, when the electricity fails.

GENTLEMAN: Machines are not perfect either. They were invented by man and they've all *his* faults!

LADY: Don't talk to me about the faults of men! Oh la la! I know all about that, they're no better than the women, they're all alike, nothing to choose between them.

GENTLEMAN: Of course. So why expect a man to do a job even a machine can't do...

LADY: I admit I'd never thought of that... yes, when you really come to think about it, it's possible after all, why not?...

GENTLEMAN: You see, Madame, mankind's future's in the future. It's just the opposite for animals and plants... But we mustn't think of the machine as a *Deus ex machina* who'll take the place of God and progress without the slightest effort on our part. On the contrary, Madame...

LADY: I never said we should!

GENTLEMAN: On the contrary, I say, man is still the best human machine! It's man who controls the machine... because he's the mind.

LADY: Now *you've* said it.

GENTLEMAN: ... and a machine's just a machine, except for the calculating machine, which calculates by itself...

LADY: That's very true, it calculates by itself, what you say is perfectly correct...

GENTLEMAN: It's just the exception that proves the rule... Look here, just now we were talking about oil and candles. In those days an egg cost a sou and not a sou more!...

LADY: Impossible!

GENTLEMAN: Believe it or not!...

LADY: It's not that I doubt your word!

GENTLEMAN: You could dine for twenty sous, food cost nothing then...

LADY: It's a different story now!

GENTLEMAN: ... You could have a good pair of shoes, good leather too, for three francs seventy-five centimes... Young folk today don't know what that means!

LADY: They don't know when they're well-off! The young are

so ungrateful!

GENTLEMAN: Nowadays everything's a thousand times dearer. So how can we really maintain that the machine's a happy invention and progress a good thing?

LADY: We can't, of course!

GENTLEMAN: You'll probably say that progress can be good or bad, like Jews or Germans or films!...

LADY: Oh no, I wouldn't say a thing like that!

GENTLEMAN: Why not? You could if you liked, you've a right to, haven't you?

LADY: Of course I have!...

GENTLEMAN: I respect everyone's right to an opinion. My ideas are up-to-date. After all there has been a French Revolution, and the Crusades, and the Inquisition, and Kaiser William, the Popes, the Renaissance, Louis XIV and all that trouble for nothing!... We've paid dearly enough for the right to say whatever comes into our heads, without having people make fun of us...

LADY: We certainly have!... This land's our home!... We won't have anyone come and upset us in our own place...

GENTLEMAN: And Joan of Arc? Have you ever wondered what *she* would say, if she could see all this?

LADY: That's a question I've asked myself more than once!

GENTLEMAN: Radio!... And *she* used to live in an old cottage! With all these modern transformations, she wouldn't know it any more!

LADY: Oh no, she certainly wouldn't know it if she saw it now!

GENTLEMAN: And yet, perhaps she would after all!

LADY: Yes, you're right, perhaps she would after all!

GENTLEMAN: To think she was burnt alive by those Englishmen and then they became our allies...

LADY: Who'd ever have thought it?

GENTLEMAN: There are *some* good Englishmen too...

LADY: But they're mostly bad!

GENTLEMAN: You needn't think the Corsicans are any better!

LADY: That's not what I meant!...

GENTLEMAN: At least they serve one good purpose. All French postmen are Corsican. Who'd bring us our mail if there weren't any postmen!

LADY: They're a necessary evil.

GENTLEMAN: Evil is never necessary.

LADY: How right you are, that's very true!

GENTLEMAN: Don't think I look down on a postman's profession.

LADY: Every profession has its points.

GENTLEMAN: [*rising to his feet*] Madame, that is a profound observation! It deserves to pass into the language as a proverb. Allow me to congratulate you... [*He kisses her hand.*] Here is the *Croix d'honneur*. [*He pins a medal on the LADY's bosom.*]

LADY: [*embarrassed*] Oh, Monsieur!... After all, I'm only a woman!... But if you really mean it!

GENTLEMAN: I promise you I do, Madame. The Truth may spring from any brain...

LADY: Flatterer!

GENTLEMAN: [*sitting down again*] Madame, you've laid your finger on the principal vice of our society, which I detest and condemn in its entirety, without wishing to cut myself off from it...

LADY: You must never do that.

GENTLEMAN: Our society, Madame, no longer respects a profession. You've only to see how the country people stream into our sprawling towns...

LADY: Yes, Monsieur, I see.

GENTLEMAN: ... When there's no respect for a profession, there's none for a child, and the child, if you don't find I express myself too strongly, is the father of the man.

LADY: Quite true.

GENTLEMAN: Perhaps too the child has forgotten how to win respect!

LADY: Perhaps.

GENTLEMAN: And yet we ought to respect a child, for if there weren't any children, the human race would very soon die out.

LADY: That's what I was thinking!...

GENTLEMAN: Loss of respect for one thing leads to another and in the end you don't even respect your own word, when you give it.

LADY: It's terrible!

GENTLEMAN: It's all the more serious when you think that the Word is divine, like the Word of God, we've no right to take it lightly...

LADY: I agree with you perfectly. That's exactly why I wanted to be sure my daughter had a sound education and a respectable profession, so she can stand on her own feet, earn an honourable living and learn to respect others by starting with herself.

GENTLEMAN: You've been very wise. What has she been doing?

LADY: She's gone a long way with her studies. I've always longed for her to be a typist. So has she. She's just got her diploma. She's going to join a firm that deals in fraudulent transactions...

GENTLEMAN: She must be very proud and happy.

LADY: She's dancing for joy from morning to night. She's worked so hard, poor little soul!

GENTLEMAN: Now she's won the reward for her labours.

LADY: It only remains for me now to find her a good husband.

GENTLEMAN: She's a fine girl.

LADY: [looking out into the wings] Well now, there is my daughter just coming. I'll introduce you to her.

[The LADY's daughter comes in. She is a man, about thirty years old, robust and virile, with a bushy black moustache, wearing a grey suit.]

GENTLEMAID: Good morning, Mummy.

[A very strong masculine voice. The gentleman-daughter kisses the LADY.]

GENTLEMAN: She's the spitting image of you, Madame.

LADY: [to GENTLEMAID] Go and say good-morning to the gentleman.

GENTLEMAID: [curtseying first] Good-morning, Monsieur!

GENTLEMAN: Good-morning, my dear! [*To the* LADY:] She's really very well brought-up. How old is she?

LADY: Ninety-three!

GENTLEMAN: She's passed her majority then?

LADY: No. She owes us eighty years, so that makes her only thirteen.

GENTLEMAN: They'll pass, you know, as quickly as the others! [*To the* GENTLEMAID:] Well now, so you're a minor?

GENTLEMAID: [*in a very powerful voice*] Yes, but don't forget: Many a minor mates a major!

[*The* GENTLEMAN *and the* LADY *rise to their feet horrified. They all look at each other petrified, the* LADY *with clasped hands.*]

CURTAIN